Sabine Baring-Gould

In the Roar of the Sea

A Tale of the Cornish Coast. Vol. III

Sabine Baring-Gould

In the Roar of the Sea
A Tale of the Cornish Coast. Vol. III

ISBN/EAN: 9783744734622

Printed in Europe, USA, Canada, Australia, Japan

Cover: Foto ©Andreas Hilbeck / pixelio.de

More available books at **www.hansebooks.com**

IN THE

ROAR OF THE SEA

A Tale of the Cornish Coast

BY

S. BARING-GOULD,

AUTHOR OF

"MEHALAH," "URITH," ETC.

IN THREE VOLUMES

VOL. III.

Methuen & Co.

18, BURY STREET, LONDON, W.C.

1892

IN THE ROAR OF THE SEA.

———◦⋈◦———

CHAPTER XXXVII.

BRUISED NOT BROKEN.

"COME with me, uncle," said Judith.

"My dear, I will follow you like a dog, anywhere."

" I want to go to the rectory."

" To the rectory !   At this time of night ? "

" At once."

When the down was left, then there was no longer necessity for hiding the lantern, as they were within lanes, and the light would not be seen at sea.

The distance to the parsonage was not great, and the little party were soon there, but were somewhat puzzled how to find the door, owing to the radical transformation of the approaches effected by the new rector.

Mr. Desiderius Mules was not in bed. He was in

his study, without his collar and necktie, smoking, and composing a sermon. It is not only *lucus* which is derived from *non lucendo.* A study in many a house is equally misnamed. In that of Mr. Mules' house it had some claim perhaps to its title, for in it once a week Mr. Desiderius cudgelled his brains how to impart form to an incoate mass of notes; but it hardly deserved its name as a place where the brain was exercised in absorption of information. The present study was the old pantry. The old study had been occupied by a man of reading and of thought. Perhaps it was not unsuitable that the pantry should become Mr. Mules' study, that where the maid had emptied her slop-water, after cleaning forks and plates, should be the place for the making of the theological slop-water that was to be poured forth on the Sunday. But, what a word has been here employed—theological —another *lucus a non lucendo,* for there was nothing of theology proper in the stuff compounded by Mr. Mules. We shall best be able to judge by observing him engaged on his sermon for Sunday.

In his mouth was a pipe, on the table a jar of birds'-eye. *Item :* a tumbler of weak brandy and water to moisten his lips with occasionally. It was weak. Mr. Mules never took a drop more than was good for him. Before him were arranged, in a circle, his materials for composition. On his extreme left was what he termed his Treacle-pot. That was a volume of unctuous piety. Then came his Dish of Flummery. That was a volume of ornate discourses by a crack lady's preacher. Next his Spice-box. That was a little store of anecdotes, illustrations, and pungent sayings. Pearson on the Creed, Bishop Andrews, no work of solid divinity was to be found either on his table or on his shelves. A Commentary was outspread, and a Concordance.

The Reverend Desiderius Mules sipped his brandy and water, took a long whiff at his pipe, and then wrote his text. Then he turned to his Commentary, and extracted from it junks of moralization upon his text and on other texts which his Concordance told him more or less had to do with his head text. Then he peppered his paper well over with quotations, those in six lines preferred to those in three, and those in one only despised as unprofitable.

" Now," said the manufacturer of the sermon, " I

must have a little treacle. I suppose those bumpkins will like it, but not much; I hate it myself. It is ridiculous! And I can dish up a trifle of flummery in here and there conveniently, and—let me see—I'll work up to a story near the tail somehow. But what heading shall I give my discourse? 'Pon my word, I don't know what its subject is. We'll call it 'General Piety.' That will do admirably—yes, 'General Piety.' Come in! Who's there?"

A servant entered, and said that there were Mr. Menaida and the lady that had been married that morning at the door wanting to speak with him. Should she show them into the study?

Mr. Mules looked at his brandy and water, then at his array of material for composition, and then at his neckerchief on the floor, and said, "No—into the drawing-room." The maid was told to light candles for them. He would put on his collar and be with them shortly. So the sermon had to be laid aside.

Presently Mr. Desiderius Mules entered his drawing-room, where Judith, Uncle Zachie, and Jamie were awaiting him.

"A late visit, but always welcome," said the rector.

"Sorry I kept you waiting, but I was *en déshabille*. What can I do for you now, eh?"

Judith was composed; she had formed her resolution. She said, "You married me this morning when I was unconscious. I answered but one of your questions. Will you get your Prayer Book, and I will make my responses to all those questions you put to me when I was in a dead faint."

"Oh, not necessary. Sign the register, and it is all right. Silence gives consent you know."

"I wish it otherwise, particularly, and then you can judge for yourself whether silence gave consent."

Mr. Desiderius Mules ran back into his study, pulled a whiff at his pipe to prevent the fire from going out, moistened his untempered clay with brandy and water, and came back again with a book of Common Prayer.

"Here we are," said he. "'Wilt thou have this man,' and so on—you answered to that, I believe. Then comes, 'I, Judith, take thee, Curll, to my wedded husband'—you were indistinct over that, I believe."

"I remember nothing about it. Now I will give you my intention distinctly. I will *not* take Curll

Coppinger to my wedded husband, and thereto I will never give my troth—so help me, God."

"Goodness gracious!" exclaimed the rector. "You put me in a queer position. I married you, and you can't undo what is done. You have the ring on your finger."

"No—here it is. I return it."

"I refuse to take it. I have nothing whatever to do with the ring. Captain Coppinger put it on your hand."

"When I was unconscious."

"But am I to be choused out of my fee, as out of other things?"

"You shall have your fee. Do not concern yourself about that. I refuse to consider myself married. I refuse to sign the register. No man shall force me to it, and if it comes to law, here are witnesses—you yourself are a witness—that I was unconscious when you married me."

"I shall get into trouble. This is a very unpleasant state of affairs."

"It is more unpleasant for me than for you," said Judith.

"It is a most awkward complication. Never heard of such a case before. Don't you think that after a good night's rest and a good supper—and let me advise a stiff glass of something warm—taken medicinally, you understand—that you will come round to a better mind."

"To another mind I shall not come round. I suppose I am half married—never by my will shall that half be made into a whole."

"And what do you want me to do?" asked Mr. Mules, thoroughly put out of his self-possession by this extraordinary scene.

"Nothing," answered Judith, "save to bear testimony that I utterly and entirely refuse to complete the marriage which was half done, by answering with assent to those questions which I failed to answer in church because I fainted, and to wear the ring which was fixed on me when I was insensible, and to sign the register now that I am in full possession of my wits. We will detain you no longer."

Judith left along with Jamie and Mr. Menaida, and Mr. Mules returned to his sermon. He pulled at his pipe till the almost expired fire was rekindled into glow, and he mixed himself a little more brandy and water. Then, with his pipe in the corner of his mouth, he looked at his discourse. It did not quite please him; it was undigested.

"Dear me!" said Mr. Desiderius; "my mind is all of a whirl, and I can do nothing to this now. It must go as it is—yet, stay, I'll change the title. 'General Piety' is rather pointless. I'll call it 'Practical Piety.'"

Judith returned to Pentyre Glaze. She was satisfied with what she had done; anger and indignation were in her heart. The man to whom she had given her hand had enlisted her poor brother in the wicked work of luring unfortunate sailors to their destruction. She could hardly conceive of anything more diabolical than this form of wrecking; her Jamie was involved in the crime of drawing men to their death. A ship had been wrecked—she knew that by the minute guns—and if lives were lost from it, the guilt in a measure rested on the head of Jamie. But for her intervention, he would have been taken in the act of showing lights to mislead mariners, and would certainly have been brought before magistrates and most probably have been imprisoned. The thought that her brother, the son of such a father, should have escaped this disgrace through an accident only, and that he had been subjected to the risk by Coppinger, filled her veins with liquid fire. Thenceforth there could be nothing between her and Captain Cruel, save, on her part, antipathy, resentment and contempt. His passion for her must cool or chafe itself away. She would never yield to him a hair's breadth.

Judith threw herself on her bed, in her clothes. She could not sleep. Wrath against Coppinger seethed in her young heart. Concerned she was for the wrecked, but concern for them was overlapped by fiery indignation against the wrecker. There was also in her breast self-reproach. She had not accepted as final her father's judgment on the man. She had allowed Coppinger's admiration of herself to move her from a position of uncompromising hostility, and to awake in her suspicions that her dear, dear father might have been mistaken, and that the man he condemned might not be so guilty as he supposed.

As she lay tossing on her bed, turning from side to side, her face now flaming, then white, she heard a noise in the house. She sat up on her bed and listened. There was now no light in the room, and she would not go into that of her aunt to borrow one. Miss Trevisa might be asleep, and would be vexed to be disturbed. Moreover, resentment against her aunt for having forced her into the marriage was strong in the girl's heart, and she had no wish to enter into any communications with her.

So she sat on her bed listening. There was certainly disturbance below. What was the meaning of it?

Presently she heard her aunt's voice downstairs. She was, therefore, not asleep in her room.

Thereupon Judith descended the stairs to the hall. There she found Captain Coppinger being carried to his bedroom by two men, whilst Miss Trevisa held a light. He was streaming with water that made pools on the floor.

"What is the matter? Is he hurt? Is he hurt seriously?" she asked, her woman's sympathy at once aroused by the sight of suffering.

"He has had a bad fall," replied her aunt. "He went to a wreck that has been cast on Doom Bar, to help to save the unfortunate, and save what they value equally with their lives—their goods, and he was washed overboard, fell into the sea, and was dashed against the boat. Yes, he is injured. No bones broken *this* time. This time he had to do with the sea and with men. But he is badly bruised. Go on," she said to those who were conveying Coppinger. "He is in pain; do you not see this as you stand there? Lay him on his bed and remove his clothes. He is drenched to the skin. I will brew him a posset."

"May I help you, aunt?"

"I can do it myself."

Judith remained with Miss Trevisa. She said nothing to her till the posset was ready. Then she offered to carry it to her husband.

"As you will: here it is," said Aunt Dionysia.

Thereupon Judith took the draught, and went with it to Captain Coppinger's room. He was in his bed. No one was with him, but a candle burned on the table.

"You have come to me, Judith?" he said, with glad surprise.

"Yes — I have brought you the posset. Drink it out to the last drop."

She handed it to him; and he took the hot caudle.

"I need not finish the bowl?" he asked.

" Yes—to the last drop."

He complied, and then suddenly withdrew the vessel from his lips.   " What is this at the bottom—a ring ? "

He extracted a plain gold ring from the bowl.

" What is the meaning of this ?   It is a wedding-ring."

" Yes—mine."

" It is early to lose it."

" I threw it in."

" You—Judith—why ? "

" I return it to you."

He raised himself on one elbow and looked at her fixedly, with threatening eyes.

" What is the meaning of this ? "

" That ring was put on my finger when I was un-conscious.   Wait till I accept it freely."

" But, Judith, the wedding is over."

" Only a half wedding."

" Well, well, it shall soon be a whole one.   We will have the register signed to-morrow."

Judith shook her head.

" You are acting strangely to-night," said he.

" Answer me," said Judith.   " Did you not send out

Jamie with a light to mislead the sailors, and draw them on to Doom Bar ?"

"Jamie again ! " exclaimed Coppinger, impatiently.

"Yes, I have to consider for Jamie. Answer me, did you not send him——"

He burst in angrily. "If you will. Yes, he took the light to the shore. I knew there was a wreck. When a ship is in distress she must have a light."

"You are not speaking the truth. Answer me—did you go on board the wrecked vessel to save those who were cast away ? "

"They would not have been saved without me. They had lost their heads—every one."

"Captain Coppinger," said Judith, "I have lost all trust in you. I return you the ring which I will never wear. I have been to see the rector and have told him that I refuse you, and that I will never sign the register."

"I will force the ring on to your finger," said Coppinger.

"You are a man, stronger than I, but I can defend myself, as you know to your cost. Half married we are, and so must remain, and never, never shall we be more than that."

Then she left the room, and Coppinger dashed the posset cup to the ground, but held the ring and turned it in his fingers, and the light flickered on it, a red-gold ring like that red-gold hair that was about his throat.

CHAPTER XXXVIII.

A CHANGE OF WIND.

AFTER many years of separation, father and son were together once more. Early in the morning after the wreck on Doom Bar, Oliver Menaida appeared at his father's cottage, bruised and wet through, but in health and with his purse in hand.

When he had gone overboard with the wrecker, the tide was falling and he had been left on the sands of the Bar, where he had spent a cold and miserable night, with only the satisfaction to warm him that his life and his money were his. He was not floating, like Wyvill, a headless trunk, nor was he without his pouch that contained his gold and valuable papers.

Mr. Menaida was roused from sleep very early to admit Oliver. The young man had recognized where

he was, as soon as sufficient light was in the sky, and
he had been carried across the estuary of the Camel by
one of the boats that was engaged in clearing the
wreck, under the direction of the captain of the coastguard.   Three men only had been arrested on the
wrecked vessel, three of those who had boarded her for
plunder; all the rest had effected their escape, and it
was questionable whether these three could be brought
to justice, as they protested they had come from shore
as salvors.   They had heard the signals of distress and
had put off to do what they could for those who were
in jeopardy.   No law forbad men coming to the assistance of the wrecked.   It could not be proved that they
had laid their hands on, and kept for their own use, any
of the goods of the passengers or any of the cargo of
the vessel.   It was true that from some of the women
their purses had been exacted, but the men taken
professed their innocence of having done this, and the
man who had made the demand—there was but one—
had disappeared.   Unhappily he had not been secured.

It was a question also whether proceedings could be
taken relative to the exhibition of lights that had mis-
guided the merchantman.   The coastguard had come

on Mr. Menaida and Judith on the downs with a light, but he was conducting her to her new home, and there could be entertained against them no suspicion of having acted with evil intent.

"Do you know, father," said Oliver, after he was rested, had slept and fed, "I am pretty sure that the scoundrel who attacked me was Captain Coppinger. I cannot swear. It is many years now since I heard his voice, and when I did hear it in former years, it was but occasionally. What made me suspect at the time that I was struggling with Captain Cruel was that he had my head back over the gunwale, and called for an axe, swearing that he would treat me like Wyvill. That story was new when I left home, and folk said that Coppinger had killed the man."

Mr. Menaida fidgeted.

"That was the man who was at the head of the entire gang. He it was who issued the orders which the rest obeyed; and he, moreover, was the man who required the passengers to deliver up their purses and valuables before he allowed them to enter the boat."

"Between ourselves," said Uncle Zachie, rubbing his chin and screwing up his mouth—"between you and me and the poker, I have no doubt about it, and I could bring his neck into the halter if I chose."

" Then why do you not do so, father? The ruffian would not have scrupled to hack off my head, had an axe been handy, or had I waited till he had got hold of one."

Mr. Menaida shook his head.

" There are a deal of things that belong to all things," he said. " I was on the down with my little pet and idol, Judith, and we had the lantern, and it was that lantern that proved fatal to your vessel."

" What, father! we owe our wreck to you?"

" No—and yet it must be suffered to be so supposed, I must allow many hard words to be rapped out against me, my want of consideration, my scatterbrainedness. I admit that I am not a Solomon, but I should not be such an ass—such a criminal—as on a night like the last to walk over the downs above the cliffs with a lantern. Nevertheless, I cannot clear myself."

" Why not?"

" Because of Judith."

" I do not understand."

" I was escorting her home—to her husband's——"

" Is she married ? "

" 'Pon my word I can't say—half-and-half."

" I do not understand you."

" I will explain later," said Mr. Menaida. " It's a perplexing question ; and, though I was brought up at the law, upon my word I can't say how the law would stand in the matter."

" But how about the false lights ? "

" I am coming to that. When the Preventive men came on us, led by Scantlebray—and why he was with them, and what concern it was of his, I don't know— when the guard found us, it is true Judith had the lantern, but it was under her cloak."

" We, however, saw the light for some time."

" Yes—but neither she nor I showed it. We had not brought a light with us. We knew that it would be wrong to do so ; but we came on some one driving an ass with the lantern affixed to the head of the brute."

" Then say so."

" I cannot. That person was Judith's brother."

" But he is an idiot."

" He was sent out with the light."

"Well, then, that person who sent him will be punished, and the silly boy will come off scot free."

"I cannot. He who sent the boy was Judith's husband."

"Judith's husband! Who is that?"

"Captain Coppinger."

"Well, what of that? The man is a double-dyed villain. He ought to be brought to justice. Consider the crimes of which he has been guilty. Consider what he has done this past night. I cannot see, father, that merely because you esteem a young person, who may be very estimable, we should let a consummate scoundrel go free, solely because he is her husband. He has brought a fine ship to wreck, he has produced much wretchedness and alarm. Indeed, he has been the occasion of some lives being lost, for one or two of the sailors, thinking we were going to Davy Jones' locker, got drunk and were carried overboard. Then, consider, he robbed some of the unhappy, frightened women as they were escaping. Bless me!"—Oliver sprang up and paced the room—"it makes my blood seethe. The fellow deserves no consideration. Give him up to justice. Let him be hung or transported."

Mr. Menaida passed his hand through his hair, and lit his pipe.

"'Pon my word," said he, " there's a good deal to be said on your side—and yet—— "

"There is everything to be said on my side," urged Oliver, with vehemence. "The man is engaged in his nefarious traffic. Winter is setting in. He will wreck other vessels as well, and if you spare him now, then the guilt of causing the destruction of other vessels, and the loss of more lives will rest in a measure on you."

"And yet," pleaded Menaida senior, " I don't know. I don't like—you see—— "

"You are moved by a little sentiment for Miss Judith Trevisa, or—I beg her pardon—Mrs. Cruel Coppinger. But it is a mistake, father. If you had had this sentimental regard for her, and value for her, you should not have suffered her to marry such a scoundrel past re-demption."

"I could not help it. I told her that the man was bad—that is to say, I believed he was a smuggler, and that he was generally credited with being a wrecker as well. But there were other influences, other forces, at work. I could not help it."

"The sooner we can rid her of this villain the better," persisted Oliver. "I cannot share your scruples, father."

Then the door opened and Judith entered.

Oliver stood up. He had re-seated himself on the opposite side of the fire to his father, after the ebullition of wrath that had made him pace the room.

He saw before him a delicate, girlish figure—a child in size and in innocence of face, but with a woman's force of character in the brow, clear eyes, and set mouth. She was very white, her golden hair was spread out about her face, blown by the wind—it was a veritable halo, such as is worn by an angel of da Fiesole or the Venus of Botticelli. Her long, slender, white throat was bare, she had short sleeves to the elbows, and bare arms. Her stockings were white, under her dark blue gown.

Oliver Menaida had spent a good many years in Portugal, and had seen flat faces, sallow complexions, and dark hair—women without delicacy of tone, and grace of figure; and on his return to England the first woman he saw was Judith. This little, pale, red-gold-headed creature was wonderful to him with her iridescent eyes full of a soul that made them sparkle and change colour with every change of emotion in the heart and of thought in the busy brain.

Oliver was a fine man, tall, with a bright and honest face, fair hair, and blue eyes. He started back from his seat, and looked attentively at this child-bride who entered his father's cottage. He knew at once who she was, from the descriptions he had received of her from his father, in letters from home.

He did not understand how she had become the wife of Cruel Coppinger. He had not heard the story from his father, still less could he comprehend the enigmatical words of his father relative to her half-and-half marriage. As now he looked on this little figure, that breathed an atmosphere of perfect purity, of white innocence, and yet not mixed with that weakness which so often characterizes innocence ; on the contrary, blended with a strength and force beyond her years. Oliver's heart rose with a bound, and smote against his ribs. He was overcome with a qualm of infinite pity for this poor little fragile being, whose life was linked with that of one so ruthless as Coppinger. Looking at that anxious face, at those lustrous eyes, set in lids that were reddened with weeping, he knew that the iron had entered into her soul, that she had suffered, and was suffering then; nay, more, that the life opening before her would be one of almost unrelieved contrariety and sorrow.

At once he understood his father's hesitation when he urged him not to increase the load of shame and trouble that lay on her.   He could not withdraw his eyes from Judith.   She was to him a vision so wonderful, so strange, so thrilling, so full of appeal to his admiration and to his chivalry.

"Here, Ju! Here is my Oliver of whom I have told you so much," said Menaida, running up to Judith. "Oliver, boy, she has read your letters, and I believe they gave her almost as great pleasure as they did to me. She was always interested in you—I mean, ever since she came into my house—and we have talked together about you; and upon my word, it really seemed as if you were to her as a brother."

A faint smile came on Judith's face; she held out her hand and said—

"Yes; I have come to love your dear father, who has been to me so kind, and to Jamie also; he has been full of thought—I mean kindness.   What has interested him has interested me. I call him uncle, so I will call you cousin. May it be so?"

He touched her hand, he did not dare to grasp the frail, slender white hand. But as he touched it, there boiled up in his heart a rage against Coppinger, that he—this man steeped in iniquity—should have obtained possession of a pearl set in ruddy gold—a pearl that he was, so thought Oliver, incapable of appreciating.

"How came you here?" asked Judith. "Your father has been expecting you some time, but not so soon."

"I am come off the wreck."

She started back and looked fixedly on him.

"What—you were wrecked?—in that ship, last night?"

"Yes. After the fog lifted we were quite lost as to where we were, and ran aground."

"What led you astray?"

"Our own bewilderment and ignorance as to where we were."

"And you got ashore?"

"Yes. I was put across by the Preventive men. I spent half the night on Doom Bar.

" Were any lives lost ? "

" Only those lost their lives who threw them away. Some tipsy sailors, who got at the spirits and drank themselves drunk."

" And—did any others—I mean did any wreckers come to your ship ? "

" Salvors ?　Yes ; salvors came to save what could be saved.　That is always so."

Judith drew a long breath of relief; but she could not forget Jamie and the ass.

" You were not led astray by false lights ? "

" Any lights we might have seen were sure to lead us astray, as we did not in the least know where we were."

"Thank you," said Judith.　Then she turned to Uncle Zachie.　" I have a favour to ask of you."

" Anything you ask I will do."

" It is to let Jamie live here.　He is more likely to be well employed, less likely to get in wrong courses, than at the Glaze.　Alas ! I cannot be with him always and everywhere, and I cannot trust him there.　Here he has his occupation ; he can help you with the birds. There he has nothing, and the men he meets are not

such as I desire that he should associate with. Besides
—you know, uncle, what occurred last night, and why I
am anxious to get him away."

"Yes," answered the old man; "I'll do my best. He
shall be welcome here."

"Moreover, Captain Coppinger dislikes him. He
might in a fit of anger maltreat him; I cannot say that
he *would*, but he makes no concealment of his dis-
like."

"Send Jamie here."

"And then I can come every day and see him, how
he is getting on, and can encourage him with his work,
and give him his lessons as usual."

"It will always be a delight to me to have you
here."

"And to me—to come." She might have said, "to
be away from Pentyre," but she refrained from saying
that.

With a faint smile—a smile that was but the twinkle
of a tear—she held out her hand to say farewell.

Uncle Zachie clasped it, and then, suddenly, she bent
and kissed his hand.

"You must not do that," said he, hastily.

She looked piteously into his eyes, and said in a whisper that he alone could hear, " I am so lonely."

When she was gone the old man returned to the ingle nook and resumed his pipe. He did not speak, but every now and then he put one finger furtively to his cheek, wiped off something, and drew very vigorous whiffs of tobacco.

Nor was Oliver inclined to speak; he gazed dreamily into the fire, with contracted brows, and hands that were clenched.

A quarter of an hour thus passed. Then Oliver looked up at his father, and said—

" There is worse wrecking than that of ships. Can nothing be done for this poor little craft, drifting in fog —aimless, and going on to the rocks? "

Uncle Zachie again wiped his cheek, and in his thoughtlessness wiped it with the bowl of his pipe and burnt himself. He shook his head.

" Now tell me what you meant when you said she was but half married," said Oliver.

Then his father related to him the circumstances of Judith's forced engagement, and of the incomplete marriage of the day before.

"By my soul!" exclaimed Oliver, "he must—he shall not treat her as he did our vessel."

"Oh, Oliver! If I had had my way—I had designed her for you."

"For me!"

Oliver bent his head and looked hard into the fire, where strange forms of light were dancing—dancing and disappearing.

Then Mr. Menaida said, between his whiffs : "Surely a change of wind, Oliver. A little while ago, and she was not to be considered : justice above all, and Judith sacrificed, if need be. Now it is Judith above all.'

"Yes," musingly, "above all."

CHAPTER XXXIX.

A FIRST LIE.

As a faithful, as a loving wife almost, did Judith attend to Coppinger for the day or two before he was himself again. He had been bruised, that was all. The waves had driven him against the boat, and he had been struck by an oar; but the very fact that he was driven against the boat had proved his salvation, for he was drawn on board, and his own men carried him swiftly to the bank, and, finding him unable to walk, conveyed him home.

On reaching home a worse blow than that of the oar had struck him, and struck him on the heart, and it was dealt him by his wife. She bade him put away from him for ever the expectation, the hope, of her becoming his in more than name.

Pain and disappointment made him irritable. He broke out into angry complaint, and Judith had much to endure. She did not answer him. She had told him her purpose, and she would neither be bullied nor cajoled to alter it.

Judith had much time to herself; she wandered through the rooms of Pentyre during the day without encountering any one, and then strolled on the cliffs; wherever she went she carried her trouble with her, gnawing at her heart. There was no deliverance for her, and she did not turn her mind in that direction. She would remain what she was—Coppinger's half-wife, a wife without a wedding ring, united to him by a most dubiously legal ceremony. She bore his name, she was content to do that; she must bear with his love turned to fury by disappointment. She would do that till it died away before her firm and unchangeable opposition.

"What will be said," growled Coppinger, "when it is seen that you wear no ring?"

"I will wear my mother's, and turn the stone within," answered Judith, "then it will be like our marriage, a semblance, nothing more."

She did appear next day with a ring. When the hand was closed it looked like a plain gold wedding-hoop. When she opened and turned her hand, it was apparent that within was a small brilliant. A modest ring, a very inexpensive one, that her father had given to her mother as a guard. Modest and inexpensive because his purse could afford no better; not because he would not have given her the best diamonds available, had he possessed the means to purchase them.

This ring had been removed from the dead finger of her mother, and Mr. Peter Trevisa had preserved it as a present for the daughter.

Almost every day Judith went to Polzeath to give lessons to Jamie, and to see how the boy was going on. Jamie was happy with Mr. Menaida, he liked a little desultory work, and Oliver was kind to him, took him walks, and talked to him of scenes in Portugal.

Very often, indeed, did Judith, when she arrived, find Oliver at his father's. He would sometimes sit through the lesson, often attend her back to the gate of Pentyre. His conduct towards her was deferential, tinged with pity. She could see in his eyes, read in his manner of address, that he knew her story, and grieved for her, and would do anything he could to release her from her place of torment, if he knew how. But he never spoke to her of Coppinger, never of her marriage, and the peculiar features that attended it. She often ventured on the topic of the wreck, and he saw that she was probing him to discover the truth concerning it, but he on no occasion allowed himself to say anything that could give her reason to believe her husband was the cause of the ship being lost, nor did he tell her of his own desperate conflict with the wrecker captain on board the vessel.

He was a pleasant companion, cheerful and entertaining. Having been abroad, though not having travelled widely, he could tell much about Portugal, and something about Spain. Judith's eager mind was greedy after information, and it diverted her thoughts from painful topics to hear and talk about orange and lemon groves, the vineyards, the flower-gardens, the manners and customs of the people of Portugal, to see sketches of interesting places, and of the costumes of the peasantry. What drew her to Oliver especially was, however, his consideration for Jamie, to whom he was always kind, and whom he was disposed to amuse.

The wreck of the merchantman on Doom Bar had caused a great commotion among the inhabitants of Cornwall. All the gentry, clergy, and the farmers and yeomen not immediately on the coast, felt that wrecking was not only a monstrous act of inhumanity, but was a scandal to the county, and ought to be peremptorily suppressed, and those guilty of it brought to justice. It was currently reported that the merchantman from Oporto was wilfully wrecked, and that an attempt had been made to rob and plunder the passengers and the vessel. But the evidence in support of this view was of little force. The only persons who had been found with a light on the cliffs were Mr. Menaida, whom every one respected for his integrity, and Judith, the daughter of the late rector of S. Enodoc, the most strenuous and uncompromising denouncer of wrecking. No one, however malicious, could believe either to be guilty of more than imprudence.

The evidence as to the attempt of wreckers to invade the ship, and plunder it and the passengers also, broke down. One lady alone could swear that her purse had been forcibly taken from her. The Portuguese nun could hardly understand English, and though she asserted that she had been asked for money, she could not say that anything had been taken from her. It was quite possible that she had misunderstood an order given her to descend into the boat. The night had been dark, the lady who had been robbed could not swear to the identity of the man who had taken her purse, she could not even say that it was one of those who had come to the vessel, and was not one of the crew. The crew had behaved notoriously badly, some had been drunk, and it was possible that one of these fellows, flushed with spirits, had demanded and taken her money.

There were two or three S. Enodoc men arrested because found on the ship at the time, but they persisted in the declaration that, hearing signals of distress, they had kindled a light and set it in the tower window of the church as a guide to the shipwrecked, and had gone to the vessel aground on Doom Bar, with the intention of offering every assistance in their power to the castaways. They asserted that they had found the deck in confusion, the seamen drunk and lost to discipline, the passengers helpless and frightened, and that it was only owing to them that some sort of order was brought about, or attempted. The arrival of the coastguard interfered with their efforts to be useful.

The magistrates were constrained to dismiss the case, although possessed with the moral conviction that the matter was not as the accused represented. The only person who could have given evidence that might have consigned them to prison was Oliver, and he was not called upon to give witness.

But, although the case had broken down completely, an uneasy and angry feeling prevailed. People were not convinced that the wreck was accidental, and they believed that but for the arrival of the guard, the passengers would have been robbed and the ship looted. It was true enough that a light had been exhibited from S. Enodoc tower, but that served as a guide to those who rushed upon the wreck, and was every whit as much to their advantage as to that of the shipwrecked men. For, suppose that the crew and passengers had got off in their boats, they would have made, naturally, for the light, and who could say but that a gang of ruffians was not waiting on the shore to plunder them as they landed?

The general feeling in the county was one of vexation

that more prompt action had not been taken, or that the action taken had not been more successful. No man showed this feeling more fully than Mr. Scantlebray, who hunted with the coastguard for his own ends, and who had felt sanguine that in this case Coppinger would be caught.

That Coppinger was at the bottom of the attempt, which had been partly successful, few doubted, and yet there was not a shadow of proof against him. But that, according to common opinion, only showed how deep was his craft.

The state of Judith's mind was also one of unrest. She had a conviction seated in her heart that all was not right, and yet she had no sound cause for charging her husband with being a deliberate wrecker. Jamie had gone out with his ass and the lantern, that was true, but was Jamie's account of the affair to be relied on? When questioned he became confused. He never could be trusted to recall twenty-four hours after an event the particulars exactly as they occurred; any suggestive queries drew him aside, and without an intent to deceive he would tell what was a lie, simply because he could not distinguish between realities and fleeting impressions. She knew that if she asked him whether Coppinger had fastened the lantern to the head of his donkey, and had bidden him drive the creature slowly up and down the inequalities of the surface of the cliffs, he would assent, and say it was so; but, then, if she were to say to him, " Now, Jamie, did not Captain Coppinger tell you on no account to show the light till you reached the shore at S. Enodoc's, and then to fix it steadily," that his face would for a moment assume a vacant, then a distressed expression, and that he would finally say he believed it really was so. No reliance was to be placed on anything he said, except at the moment, and not always then. He was liable to misunderstand directions, and by a stupid perversity to act exactly contrary to the instructions given him.

Judith heard nothing of the surmises that floated in the neighbourhood, but she knew enough to be uneasy. She had been somewhat reassured by Oliver Menaida; she could see no reason why he should withhold the truth from her. Was it, then, possible after all that Captain Coppinger had gone to the rescue of the wrecked people, that he had sent the light not to mislead, but to direct them aright?

It was Judith's fate—so it seemed—to be never certain whether to think the worst of Coppinger, or to hold that he had been misjudged by her. He had been badly hurt in his attempt to rescue the crew and passengers—according to Aunt Dionysia's account. If she were to believe this story then he was deserving of respect.

Judith began to recover some of her cheerfulness, some of her freshness of looks. This was due to the abatement of her fears. Coppinger had angrily, sullenly, accepted the relation which she had assured him must subsist between them, and which could never be altered.

Aunt Dionysia was peevish and morose indeed. She had been disappointed in her hope of getting into Othello Cottage before Christmas; but she had apparently received a caution from Coppinger not to exhibit ill-will towards his wife by word or token, and she restrained herself, though with manifest effort. That sufficed Judith. She no longer looked for, cared for love from her aunt. It satisfied her if Miss Trevisa left her unmolested.

Moreover, Judith enjoyed the walk to Polzeath every

day, and, somehow, the lessons to Jamie gave her an interest that she had never found in them before. Oliver was so helpful. When Jamie was stubborn, he persuaded him with a joke or a promise to laugh and put aside his ill-humour, and attack the task once more. The little gossiping talk after the lesson with Oliver, or with Oliver and his father, was a delight to her. She looked forward to it from day to day, naturally, reasonably, for at the Glaze she had no one with whom to converse, no one with the same general interests as herself, the same knowledge of books, and pleasure in the acquisition of information.

On mountain sides there are floral zones. The rhododendron and the gentian luxuriate at a certain level, above is the zone of the blue hippatica, the soldanella, and white crocus, below is the belt of mealy primula and lilac clematis. So is it in the world of minds—they have their levels, and can only live on those levels. Transplant them to a higher or to a lower zone and they suffer, and die.

Judith found no one at Pentyre with whom she could associate with pleasure. It was only when she was at Polzeath with Uncle Zachie and Oliver that she could talk freely and feel in her element.

One day Oliver said to her, "Judith,"—for, on the understanding that they were cousins, they called each other by their Christian names—"Judith, are you going to the ball at Wadebridge after Christmas?"

"Ball, Oliver, what ball?"

"That which Mr. Mules is giving for the restoration of his church."

"I do not know. I—yes, I have heard of it; but I had clean forgotten all about it. I had rather not."

"But you must, and promise me three dances at least."

"I do not know what to say. Captain Coppinger"—she never spoke of her husband by his Christian name, never thought of him as other than Captain Coppinger. Did she think of Oliver as Mr. Menaida, junior?—"Captain Coppinger has not said anything to be about it of late. I do not wish to go. My dear father's death——"

"But the dance is after Christmas. And, you know, it is for a sacred purpose. Think, every whirl you take puts a new stone on the foundations, and every setting to your partner in quadrilles adds a pane of glass to the battered windows."

"I do not know," again said Judith, and became

grave. Her heart fluttered. She would like to be at the ball, and dance three dances with Oliver, but would Captain Coppinger suffer her? Would he expect to dance with her all the evening? If that were so, she would not like to go. "I really do not know," again she said, clasped her hands on her knees, and sighed.

"Why that sigh, Judith?"

She looked up, dropped her eyes in confusion, and said faintly, "I do not know." And that was her first lie.

CHAPTER XL.

THE DIAMOND BUTTERFLY.

POOR little fool! Shrewd in maintaining her conflict with Cruel Coppinger—always on the defensive, ever on guard, she was sliding unconsciously, without the smallest suspicion of danger, into a state that must eventually make her position more desperate and intolerable. In her inexperience she had never supposed that her own heart could be a traitor within the city walls. She took pleasure in the society of Oliver, and thought no wrong in so doing. She liked him, and would have reproached herself had she not done so.

Her relations with Coppinger remained strained. He was a good deal from home, indeed he went a cruise in his vessel, the *Black Prince*, and was.

absent for a month. He hoped that in his absence she might come to a better mind. They met when he was at home at meals, at other times not at all; he went his way, she went hers. Whether the agitation of men's minds relative to the loss of the merchant-man, and the rumours concerning the manner of its loss, had made Captain Cruel think it were well for him to absent himself for a while till they had blown away, or whether he thought that his business required his attention elsewhere, or that by being away from home his wife might be the readier to welcome him, and come out of her vantage castle, and lay down her arms, cannot be said for certain; probably all these motives combined to induce him to leave Pentyre for five or six weeks. Whilst he was away Judith was lighter in heart.

He returned shortly before Christmas, and was glad to see her more like her old self, with cheeks rounder, less livid, eyes less sunken, less like those of a hunted beast, and with a step that had resumed its elasticity. But he did not find her more disposed to receive him with affection as a husband. He thought that pro-bably some change in the monotony of life at Pentyre might be of advantage, and he somewhat eagerly entered into the scheme for the ball at Wadebridge. She had been kept to books and to the society of her father too much in days gone by, and had become whimsical and prudish. She must learn some of the enjoyments of life, and then she would cling to the man who opened to her a new sphere of happiness.

"Judith," said he, "we will certainly go to this ball. It will be a pleasant one. As it is for a charitable purpose, all the neighbourhood will be there. Squire Humphrey Prideaux of Prideaux Place, the Matthews of Roscarrock, the Molesworths of Pencarrow, and every one worth knowing in the country round for twelve miles. But you will be the queen of the ball."

Judith at first thought of appearing at the dance in her simplest evening dress; she was shy and did not desire to attract attention. Her own position was anomalous, because that of Coppinger was anomalous. He passed as a gentleman in a part of the country not very exacting that the highest culture should prevail in the upper region of society. He had means, and he owned a small estate. But no one knew whence he came, or what was the real source whence he derived his income.　Suspicion attached to him as engaged in both smuggling and wrecking, neither of which were regarded as professions consonant with gentility.　The result of this uncertainty relative to Coppinger was that he was not received into the best society.　The gentlemen knew him and greeted him in the hunting-field, and would dine with him at his house.　The ladies, of course, had never been invited, because he was an unmarried man.　The gentlemen probably had dealings with him about which they said nothing to their wives. It is certain that the Bodmin wine merchant grumbled that the great houses of the North of Cornwall did not patronise him as they ought, and that no wine merchant was ever able to pick up a subsistence at Wadebridge.　Yet the country gentry were by no means given to temperance; and their cellars were being continually refilled.

It was not their interest to be on bad terms with Coppinger, one must conjecture, for they went somewhat out of their way to be civil to him.

Coppinger knew this, and thought that now he was married an opportunity had come in this charity ball, for the introduction of Judith to society, and that to the best society, and he trusted to her merits and beauty, and to his own influence with the gentlemen, to obtain for her admission to the houses of the neighbourhood. As the daughter of the Rev. Peter Trevisa, who had been universally respected, not only as a gentleman and a scholar, but also as the representative of an ancient Cornish family of untold antiquity, she had a perfect right to be received into the highest society of Cornwall, but her father had been a reserved and poor man. He did not himself care for associating with fox-hunting and sporting squires, nor would he accept invitations when he was unable to return them. Consequently Judith had gone about very little when at S. Enodoc Rectory. Moreover, she had been but a child, and was known only by name to those who lived in the neighbourhood, she was personally acquainted with none of the county people.

Captain Cruel had small doubt but that, the ice once broken, Judith would make friends, and would be warmly received. The neighbourhood was scantily peppered over with county family seats, and the families found the winters tedious, and were glad of any accession to their acquaintance, and of another house opened to them for entertainment.

If Judith were received well, and found distraction from her morbid and fantastic thoughts, then she would be grateful to him—so thought Coppinger—grateful for having brought her into a more cheerful and bright condition of life than that in which she had been reared. Following thereon, her aversion from him, or shyness towards him, would give way.

And Judith—what were her thoughts? Her mind was a little fluttered, she had to consider what to wear. At first she would go simply clad, then her aunt insisted that, as a bride, she must appear in suitable gown—that in which she had been married, not that with the two sleeves for one side, which had been laid by. Then the question of the jewellery arose. Judith did not wish to wear it, but yielded to her aunt's advice. Miss Trevisa represented to her that, having the diamonds, she ought to wear them, and that not to wear them would hurt and offend Captain Coppinger, who had given them to her. This she was reluctant to do. However, she consented to oblige and humour him in such a small matter.

The night arrived, and Judith was dressed for the ball. Never before had Coppinger seen her in evening costume, and his face beamed with pride as he looked on her in her white silk dress, with ornaments of white satiny bugles in sprigs edging throat and sleeve, and forming a rich belt about the waist. She wore the diamond butterfly in her bosom, and the two earrings to match. A little colour was in her delicately pure cheeks, brought there by excitement. She had never been at a ball before, and with an innocent, childish simplicity she wondered what Oliver Menaida would think of her in her ball dress.

Judith and Coppinger arrived somewhat late, and most of those who had taken tickets were already there. Sir William and Lady Molesworth were there, and the half-brother of Sir William, John Molesworth, rector of S. Breock, and his wife, the daughter of Sir John S. Aubyn. With the baronet and his lady had come a friend, staying with them at Pencarrow, and Lady Knighton, wife of an Indian judge. The Matthews were there ; the Tremaynes came all the way from Heligan, as owning property in S. Enodoc, and so in duty bound to support the charity ; the

Prideaux were there from Place; and many, if not all, of the gentry of various degrees who resided within twelve to fifteen miles of Wadebridge were also there.

The room was not one of any interest, it was long, had a good floor, which is the main thing considered by dancers, a gallery at one end for the instrumentalists, and a draught which circulated round the walls, and cut the throats of the old ladies who acted as wall-fruit. There was, however, a room to which they could adjourn to play cards. And many of the dowagers and old maids had brought with them little silver-linked purses in which was as much money as they had made up their minds to lose that evening.

The Dowager Lady Molesworth in a red turban was talking to Lady Knighton, a lady who had been pretty, but whose complexion had been spoiled by Indian suns. and to her Sir William was offering a cup of tea.

"You see," said Lady Knighton, "how tremulous my hand is. I have been like this for some years—indeed ever since I was in this neighbourhood before."

"I did not know you had honoured us with a visit on a previous occasion," said Sir William.

"It was very different from the present, I can assure
you," answered the lady. "Now it is voluntarily—then it
was much the contrary. Now I have come among very
dear and kind friends, then—I fell among thieves."

"Indeed!"

"It was on my return from India," said Lady
Knighton. "Look at my hand!" She held forth
her arm, and showed how it shook as with palsy.
"This hand was firm then. I even played several
games of spellikins on board ship on the voyage home,
and, Sir William, I won invariably, so steady was my
hold of the crook, so evenly did I raise each of the
little sticks. But ever since then I have had this
nervous tremor that makes me dread holding anything."

"But how came it about?" asked the baronet.

"I will tell you, but—who is that just entered the
room?" she pointed with trembling finger.

Judith had come in along with Captain Coppinger,
and stood near the door, the light of the wax candles
twinkling in her bugles, glancing in flashes from her
radiant hair. She was looking about her, and her
bosom heaved. She sought Oliver, and he was near

at hand.   A flush of pleasure sprang into her cheeks as
she caught his eye, and held out her hand.

" I demand my dance ! " said he.

" No, not the first, Oliver," she answered.

Coppinger's brows knit.

" Who is this ? " he asked.

" Oh! do you not know?   Mr. Menaida's son, Mr.
Oliver."

The two men's eyes met, their irises contracted.

" I think we have met before," said Oliver.

"That is possible," answered Captain Cruel, con-
temptuously, looking in another direction.

" When we met, I knew you without your knowing
me," pursued the young man in a voice that shook
with anger.   He had recognized the tone of the voice
that had spoken on the wreck.

"Of that I, neither, have any doubt as to its
possibility.   I do not recollect every Jack I encounter."

A moment after an idea struck him, and he turned
his head sharply, fixed his eyes on young Menaida,
and said, " Where did we meet ? "

" ' Encounter' was your word."

. " Very well—encounter ? "

" On Doom Bar."

Coppinger's colour changed. A sinister flicker came into his sombre eyes.

" Then," said he slowly, in low vibrating tones, " we shall meet again."

" Certainly, we shall meet again, and conclude our —I use your term—encounter."

Judith did not hear the conversation. She had been pounced upon by Mr. Desiderius Mules.

" Now—positively I must walk through a quadrille with you," said the rector. " This is all my affair ; it all springs from me, I arranged everything. I beat up patrons and patronesses. I stirred up the neighbour-hood. It all turns as a wheel about me as the axle. Come along, the band is beginning to play. You shall positively walk through a quadrille with me."

Mr. Mules was not the man to be put on one side, not one to accept a refusal ; he carried off the bride to the head of the room, and set her in one square.

" Look at the decorations," said Mr. Mules, " I designed them. I hope you will like the supper. I drew up the *menu*. I chose the wines, and I know they are good. The candles I got at wholesale price—because for a charity. What beautiful diamonds you are wearing. They are not paste, I suppose?"

" I believe not."

" Yet good old paste is just as irridescent as real diamonds. Where did you get them? Are they family jewels? I have heard that the Trevisas were great people at one time. Well, so were the Mules. We are really De Moels. We came in with the Conqueror. That is why I have such a remarkable Christian name, Desiderius is the French Désiré — and a Norman Christian name. Look at the wreaths of laurel and holly. How do you like them?"

" The decorations are charming."

" I am so pleased that you have come," pursued Mr. Mules. " It is your first appearance in public as Mrs. Captain Coppinger. I have been horribly uncomfortable about—you remember what. I have been afraid I had put my foot into it, and might get into hot water. But now you have come here, it is all right; it shows me that you are coming round to a sensible view, and that to-morrow you will be at the Rectory and sign the register. If inconvenient, I will run up with it under my arm to the Glaze. At what time am I likely to catch you both in? The witnesses, Miss Trevisa and Mr. Menaida, one can always get at. Perhaps you will speak to your aunt and see that she is on the spot, and I'll take the old fellow on my way home."

" Mr. Mules, we will not talk of that now."

"Come! you must see, and be introduced to, Lady Molesworth."

In the meanwhile Lady Knighton was telling her story to a party round her.

"I was returning with my two children from India; it is now some years ago. It is so sad, in the case of Indians, either the parents must part from their children, or the mother must take her children to England and be parted from her husband. I brought my little ones back to be with my husband's sister, who kindly undertook to see to them. We encountered a terrible gale as we approached this coast; do you recollect the loss of the *Andromeda* ?"

" Perfectly," answered Sir William Molesworth; " were you in that ? "

" Yes, to my cost. One of my darlings so suffered from the exposure that she died. But, really, I do not think it was the wreck of the vessel which was worst. It was not that, or not that alone, which brought this nervous tremor on me."

" I remember that case," said Sir William. " It was a very bad one, and disgraceful to our county. We have recently had an ugly story of a wreck on Doom Bar, with suspicion of evil practices; but nothing could be proved, nothing brought home to any one. In the case of the *Andromeda* there was something of the same sort."

" Yes, indeed, there were evil practices. I was robbed."

" You! surely, Lady Knighton, it was not of you that the story was told?"

" If you mean the story of the diamonds, it was," answered the Indian lady. " We had to leave the wreck, and carry all our portable valuables with us. I had a set of jewellery of Indian work given me by Sir James—well, he was only plain Mr. Knighton then. It was rather quaint in design: there was a brooch representing a butterfly, and two emeralds formed the——"

" Excuse me one moment, Lady Knighton," said Sir

William. "Here comes the new rector of S. Enodoc with the bride to introduce her to my wife. I am ashamed to say we have not made her acquaintance before."

"Bride! what—his bride?"

"Oh, no! the bride of a certain Captain Coppinger, who lives near here."

"She is pretty, very pretty; but how delicate!"

Suddenly Lady Knighton sprang to her feet, with an exclamation so shrill and startling that the dancers ceased, and the conductor of the band, thinking an accident had occurred, with his baton stopped the music. All attention was drawn to Lady Knighton, who, erect, trembling from head to foot, stood pointing with shaking finger to Judith.

"See! see! my jewels, that were torn from me! Look!" She lifted the hair, worn low over her cheeks, and displayed one ear; the lobe was torn away.

No one stirred in the ball-room; no one spoke. The fiddler stood with bow suspended over the strings, the flutist with fingers on all stops. Every eye was fixed on Judith. It was still in that room as though a ghost had passed through in winding-sheet. In this hush,

Lady Knighton approached Judith, pointing still with trembling hand.

" I demand whence comes that brooch ? where—from whom did you get those earrings? They are mine ; given me in India by my husband. They are Indian work, and not to be mistaken. They were plucked from me one awful night of wreck by a monster in human form who came to our vessel, as we sought to leave it, and robbed us of our treasures. Answer me— who gave you those jewels ? "

Judith was speechless. The lights in the room died to feeble stars. The floor rolled like a sea under her feet ; the ceiling was coming down on her.

She heard whispers, murmurs—a humming as of a swarm of bees approaching ready to settle on her and sting her. She looked round her. Every one had withdrawn from her. Mr. Desiderius Mules had released her arm, and stood back. She tried to speak, but could not. Should she make the confession which would incriminate her husband ?

Then she heard a deep man's voice, heard a step on the floor. In a moment an arm was round her, sustaining her, as she tottered.

" I gave her the jewels. I, Curll Coppinger, of Pen-tyre. If you ask where I got it, I will tell you. I bought them of Willy Mann, the pedlar. I will give you any further information you require to-morrow. Make room ; my wife is frightened."

Then, holding her, looking haughtily, threateningly, from side to side, Coppinger helped Judith along—the whole length of the ball-room—between rows of aston-ished, open-eyed, mute dancers. Near the door was a knot of gentlemen. They sprang apart, and Coppinger conveyed Judith through the door, out of the light, down the stair, into the open air.

CHAPTER XLI.

A DEADLOCK.

THE incident of the jewellery of Lady Knighton occasioned much talk. On the evening of the ball it occupied the whole conversation, as the sole topic on which tongues could run and brains work. I say tongues run and brains work, and not brains work and tongues run, for the former is the natural order in chatter. It was a subject that was thrashed by a hundred tongues of the dancers. Then it was turned over and re-thrashed. Then it was winnowed. The chaff of the tale was blown into the kitchens and servants'-halls, it drifted into taprooms, where the coachmen and grooms congregated and drank; and there it was re-thrashed and re-winnowed.

On the day following the ball the jewels were re-

turned to Lady Knighton, with a courteous letter from
Captain Coppinger, to say that he had obtained them
through the well-known Willy Mann, a pedlar who did
commissions for the neighbourhood, who travelled from
Exeter along the south coast of Devon and Cornwall,
and returned along the north coast of both counties.

Every one had made use of this fellow to do commissions, and trustworthy he had always proved. That
was not a time when there was a parcels post, and few
could afford the time and the money to run at every
requirement to the great cities, where were important
shops, when they required what could not be obtained
in small country towns. He had been employed to
match silks, to choose carpets, to bring medicines, to
select jewellery, to convey love letters.

But Willy Mann had, unfortunately, died a month
ago, having fallen off a waggon and broken his neck.

Consequently it was not possible to follow up any
further the traces of the diamond butterflies. Willy
Mann, as was well known, had been a vehicle of conveying sundry valuables from ladies who had lost money
at cards, and wanted to recoup by parting with bracelets
and brooches. That he may have received stolen goods

and valuables obtained from wrecks was also pro-bable.

So, after all the thrashing and winnowing, folks were no wiser than before, and no nearer the solution of the mystery. Some thought that Coppinger was guilty, others thought not, and others maintained a neutral position. Some again thought one thing one day and the opposite the next; and some always agreed with the last speaker's views; whereas others again always took a contrary opinion to those who discussed the matter with them.

Moreover, the matter went through a course much like a fever. It blazed out, was furious, then died away; languor ensued, and it gave symptoms of disappearing.

The general mistrust against Coppinger was deepened, certainly, and the men who had wine and spirits and tobacco through him resolved to have wine and spirits and tobacco from him, but nothing more. They would deal with him as a trader, and not acknowledge him as their social fellow. The ladies pitied Judith, they professed their respect for her; but as beds are made so must they be lain on, and as is cooked so must be eaten. She had married a man whom all mistrusted, and must suffer accordingly; one who is associated with an infected patient is certain to be shunned as much as the patient. Such is the way of the world, and we cannot alter it, as the making of that way has not been entrusted to us.

On the day following the ball, Judith did not appear at Polzeath, nor again on the day after that.

Oliver became restless. The cheerful humour, the merry mood that his father had professed were his, had deserted him. He could not endure the thought that one so innocent, so childlike as Judith, should have her fortunes linked to those of a man of whom he knew the worst. He could not, indeed, swear to his identity with the man on the wreck who had attempted to rob the passengers, and who had fought with him. He had no doubt whatever in his own mind that his adversary and assailant had been Coppinger; but he was led to this identification by nothing more tangible than the allusion made to Wyvill's death, and a certain tone of voice which he believed he recognized. The evidence was insufficient to convict him, of that Oliver was well aware. He was confident, moreover, that Coppinger

was the man who had taken the jewels from Lady
Knighton; but here again he was wholly unsupported
by any sound basis of fact on which his conviction
could maintain itself.

Towards Coppinger he felt an implacable anger, and
a keen desire for revenge. He would like to punish him
for that assault on the wreck, but chiefly for the wrongs
done to Judith. She had no champion, no protector.
His father, as he acknowledged to himself, was a broken
reed for one to lean on, a man of good intentions, but
of a confused mind, of weakness of purpose, and lack
of energy. The situation of Judith were a pitiful one,
and if she were to be rescued from it, he must rescue
her. But when he came to consider the way and
means, he found himself beset with difficulties. She
was married after a fashion. It was very questionable
whether the marriage were legal, but nevertheless it
was known through the county that a marriage had
taken place, Judith had gone to Coppinger's house, and
had appeared at the ball as his wife. If he established
before the world that the marriage was invalid, what
would she do? How would the world regard her?
Was it possible for him to bring Coppinger to justice?

Oliver went about instituting inquiries. He endeavoured to trace to their source, the rumours that circulated relative to Coppinger but always without finding anything on which he could lay hold. It was made plain to him that Captain Cruel was but the head of a great association of men, all involved in illegal practices; men engaged in smuggling, and ready to make their profit out of a wreck when a wreck fell in their way. They hung together like bees. Touch one, and the whole hive swarmed out. They screened one another, were ready to give testimony before magistrates that would exculpate whoever of the gang was accused. They evaded every attempt of the coastguard to catch them ; they laughed at the constables and magistrates. Information was passed from one to another with incredible rapidity ; they had their spies and their agents along the coast. The magistrates and country gentry, though strongly reprobating wrecking, and bitterly opposed to poaching, were of broad and generous views regarding smuggling, and the Preventive officer complained that he did not receive that support from the squirearchy which he expected and had a right to demand.

There were caves along the whole coast from Land's End to Hartland, and there were, unquestionably, stores of smuggled goods in a vast number of places, centres whence they were distributed. When a vessel engaged in the contraband trade appeared off the coast, and the guard were on the alert in one place, she ran a few miles up or down, signalled to shore, and landed her cargo before the coastguard knew where she was. They were being constantly deceived by false information, and led away in one direction whilst the contraband goods were being conveyed ashore in an opposite quarter.

Oliver learned much concerning this during the ensuing few days. He made acquaintance with the officer in command of the nearest station, and resolved to keep a close watch on Coppinger, and to do his utmost to effect his arrest. When Captain Cruel was got out of the way, then something could be done for Judith. An opportunity came in Oliver's way of learning tidings of importance, and that when he least expected it. As already said, he was wont to go about on the cliffs with Jamie, and after Judith ceased to appear at Mr. Menaida's cottage, in his unrest he took

Jamie much with him, out of consideration for Judith, who, as he was well aware, would be content to have her brother with him, and kept thereby out of mischief.

On one of these occasions he found the boy lag behind, become uneasy, and at last refuse to go further. He inquired the reason, and Jamie, in evident alarm, replied that he dare not—he had been forbidden.

" By whom ? "

" He said he would throw me over, as he did my doggie, if I came here again."

" Who did ? "

" Captain Coppinger."

" But why ? "

Jamie was frightened, and looked round.

" I mustn't say," he answered, in a whisper.

" Must not say what, Jamie ? "

" I was to let no one know about it."

" About what ? "

" I am afraid to say. He would throw me over. I found it out and showed it to Ju. I have never been down there since."

"Captain Coppinger found you somewhere, and forbade your ever going to that place again ? "

"Yes," in a faltering voice.

"And threatened to fling you over the cliffs if you did ? "

"Yes," again timidly.

Oliver said quietly, "Now run home and leave me here."

"I daren't go by myself. I did not mean to come here."

"Very well. No one has seen you. Let me see, this wall marks the spot. I will go back with you."

Oliver was unusually silent as he walked to Polzeath with Jamie. He was unwilling further to press the boy. He would probably confuse him by throwing him into a paroxysm of alarm. He had gained sufficient information for his purpose from the few words let drop. "I have never been down there since," Jamie had said. There was, then, something that Coppinger desired should not be generally known concealed between the point on the cliff where the "new-take" wall ended and the beach immediately beneath.

He took Jamie to his father, and got the old man to give him some setting up of birds to amuse and occupy him, and then returned to the cliff. It did not take him long to discover the entrance to the cave beneath, behind the curtain of slate reef, and as he penetrated this to the furthest point, he was placed in possession of one of the secrets of Coppinger and his band.

He did not tarry there, but returned home another way, musing over what he had learned, and considering what advantage he was to take of it. A very little thought satisfied him that his wisest course was to say nothing about what he had learnt, and to await the turns of fortune, and the incautiousness of the smugglers.

From this time, moreover, he discontinued his visits to the coastguard station, which was on the further side of the estuary of the Camel, and which could not well be crossed without attracting attention. There was no trusting any one, Oliver felt—the boatman who put him across was very possibly in league with the smugglers, and was a spy on those who were in communication with the officers of the Revenue.

Another reason for his cessation of visits was that, on his return to his father's house, after having explored the cave and the track in the face of the cliff

leading to it, he heard that Jamie had been taken away
by Coppinger. The Captain had been there during his
absence, and had told Mr. Menaida that Judith was
distressed at being separated from her brother, and
that, as there were reasons which made him desire
that she should forego her walks to Polzeath, he, Captain Coppinger, deemed it advisable to bring Jamie
back to Pentyre.

Oliver asked himself, when he heard this, with
some unease, whether this was due to his having
been observed with the boy on the downs near the
place from which access to the cave was had. Also,
whether the boy would be frightened at the appearance
of Captain Cruel so soon after he had approached the
forbidden spot, and, in his fear, reveal that he had
been there with Oliver and had partially betrayed the
secret.

There was another question he was also constrained
to ask himself, and it was one that made the colour
flash into his cheek. What was the particular reason
why Captain Coppinger objected to the visits of his
wife to Polzeath at that time? Was he jealous? He
recalled the flame in his eyes at the ball, when Judith

turned to him, held out her hand, and called him by
his Christian name.

From this time all communication with Pentyre
Glaze was cut off; tidings relative to Judith and
Jamie were not to be had. Judith was not seen,
Aunt Dionysia rarely, and from her nothing was to
be learned. It would hardly comport with discretion
for inquiries to be made by Oliver of the servants of
the Glaze; but his father, moved by Oliver and by his
own anxiety, did venture to go to the house and ask
after Judith. He was coldly received by Miss Trevisa,
who took the opportunity to insult him by asking if he
had come to have his bill settled, there being a small
account in his favour for Jamie. She paid him, and
sent the old fellow fuming, stamping, even swearing,
home, and as ignorant of the condition of Judith as
when he went. He had not seen Judith, nor had he
met Captain Coppinger. He had caught a glimpse
of Jamie in the yard with his donkey, but the
moment the boy saw him he dived into the stable,
and did not emerge from it till Uncle Zachie was gone.

Then Mr. Menaida, still urged by his son and by
his own feelings, incapable of action unless goaded by

these double spurs, went to the rectory to ask Mr.
Mules if he had seen Judith, and whether anything
had been done about the signatures in the register.

Mr. Desiderius was communicative. He had been
to Pentyre about the matter. He was, as he said,
"in a stew over it" himself. It was most awkward;
he had filled in as much as he could of the register,
and all that lacked were the signatures—he might say
all but that of the bride and of Mr. Menaida, for there
had been a scene. Mrs. Coppinger had come down,
and, in the presence of the Captain and her aunt, he
had expostulated with her, had pointed out to her the
awkward position in which it placed himself, the scruple
he felt at retaining the fee when the work was only half
done; how, that by appearing at the ball, she had shown
to the whole neighbourhood that she was the wife of
Captain Coppinger, and that, having done this, she
might as well append her name to the entry in the
register. Then Captain Coppinger and Miss Trevisa
had made the requisite entries, but Judith had again
calmly, but resolutely, refused.

Mr. Mules admitted there had been a scene. Mr.
Coppinger became angry, and used somewhat violent

words. But nothing that he himself could say, no representations made by her aunt, no urgency on the part of her husband could move the resolution of Judith, "which was a bit of arrant tomfoolery," said Mr. Desiderius, "and I told her so. Even that—the knowledge that she went down a peg in my estimation —even that did not move her."

"And how was she?" asked Mr. Menaida.

"Obstinate," answered the rector—"obstinate as a m—, I mean as a donkey. That is the position of affairs. We are at a deadlock."

CHAPTER XLII.

TWO LETTERS.

OLIVER MENAIDA was summoned to Bristol by the heads of the firm which he served, and he was there detained for ten days.

Whilst he was away, Uncle Zachie felt his solitude greatly. Had he had even Jamie with him he might have been content, but to be left completely alone was a trial to him, especially since he had become accustomed to having the young Trevisa in his house. He missed his music. Judith's playing had been to him an inexpressibly great delight. The old man for many years had gone on strumming and fumbling at music by great masters, incapable of executing it, and unwilling to hear it performed by incompetent instrumentalists. At length Judith had seated herself at his piano, and had brought into life all that wondrous world of melody and harmony which he had guessed at, believed in, yearned for, but never reached. And now that he was left without her to play to him, he felt like one deprived of a necessary of life.

But his unrest did not spring solely from a selfish motive. He was not at ease in his mind about her. Why did he not see her any more? Why was she confined to Pentyre? Was she ill? Was she restrained there against her will from visiting her old friends? Mr. Menaida was very unhappy because of Judith. He knew that she was resolved never to acknowledge Coppinger as her real husband; she did not love him, she shrank from him. And knowing what he did—the story of the invasion of the wreck, the fight with Oliver—he felt that there was no brutality, no crime which Coppinger was not capable of committing, and he trembled for the happiness of the poor little creature who was in his hands. Weak and irresolute though Mr. Menaida was, he was peppery and impulsive when irritated, and his temper had been roused by the manner of his reception at the Glaze, when he went there to inquire after Judith.

Whilst engaged on his birds, his hand shook, so that he could not shape them aright. When he smoked his pipe, he pulled it from between his lips every moment to growl out some remark. When he sipped his grog, he could not enjoy it. He had a tender heart, and he had become warmly attached to Judith. He firmly believed in the identification of the ruffian with whom Oliver had fought on the deck, and it was horrible to think that the poor child was at his mercy; and that she had no one to counsel and to help her.

At length he could endure the suspense no longer. One evening, after he had drunk a good many glasses of rum and water, he jumped up, put on his hat, and went off to Pentyre, determined to insist on seeing Judith.

As he approached the house he saw that the hall windows were lighted up. He knew which was Judith's room, from what she had told him of its position. There was a light in that window also. Uncle Zachie, flushed with anger against Coppinger, and with the spirits he had drunk, anxious about Judith, and resenting the way in which he had been treated, went boldly up to the front door and knocked. A maid answered his knock, and he asked to see Mrs. Coppinger. The woman hesitated, and bade him be seated in the porch. She would go and see.

Presently Miss Trevisa came, and shut the door behind her, as she emerged into the porch.

" I should like to see Mrs. Coppinger," said the old man.

" I am sorry—you cannot," answered Miss Trevisa.

" But why not ? "

" This is not a fit hour at which to call."

" May I see her if I come at any other hour ? "

" I cannot say."

" Why may I not see her ? "

" She is unwell."

" If she is unwell, then I am very certain she would be glad to see Uncle Zachie."

" Of that I am no judge, but you cannot be admitted now."

" Name the day, the hour, when I may."

" That I am not at liberty to do."

" What ails her ?—where is Jamie ? "

" Jamie is here—in good hands."

" And Judith ? "

" She is in good hands."

"In good hands!" exclaimed Mr. Menaida, " I should like to see the good, clean hands worn by any one in this house, except my dear, innocent little Judith. I must and will see her. I must know from her own lips how she is. I must see that she is happy—or at least not maltreated."

"Your words are insult to me, her aunt, and to Captain Coppinger, her husband," said Miss Trevisa, haughtily.

" Let me have a word with Captain Coppinger."

" He is not at home."

" Not at home!—I hear a great deal of noise. There must be a number of guests in the hall. Who is entertaining them, you or Judith ? "

" That is no concern of yours, Mr. Menaida."

" I do not believe that Captain Coppinger is not at home. I insist on seeing him."

"Were you to see him—you would regret it afterwards. He is not a person to receive impertinences and pass them over. You have already behaved in a most indecent manner, in encouraging my niece to visit your house, and sit, and talk, and walk with, and call by his Christian name that young fellow your son."

"Oliver!" Mr. Menaida was staggered. It had never occurred to his fuddled, yet simple mind, that the intimacy that had sprung up between the young people was capable of misinterpretation. The sense that he had laid himself open to this charge made him very angry, not with himself, but with Coppinger and with Miss Trevisa.

"I'll tell you what," said the old man. "If you will not let me in, I suppose you will not object to my writing a line to Judith."

"I have received orders to allow of no communication of any kind whatsoever between my niece and you or your house."

"You have received orders—from Coppinger?" the old man flamed with anger. "Wait a bit! There is no command issued that you are not to take a message from me to your master?"

He put his hand into his pocket, pulled out a note-book, and tore out of it a page. Then, by the light from the hall window, he scribbled on it a few lines in pencil.

"Sir!—You are a scoundrel. You bully your wife. You rob, and attempt to murder those who are ship-wrecked.

"Zachary Menaida."

"There," said the old man, "that will draw him, and I shall see him, and have it out with him."

He had wafers in his pocket-book. He wetted and sealed the note. Then he considered that he had not said enough, so he opened the page again, and added— "I shall tell all the world what I know about you." Then he fastened the note again and directed it. But as it suddenly occurred to him that Captain Coppinger might refuse to open the letter, he added on the out-side—"The contents I know by heart; and shall proclaim them on the house-tops." He thrust the note into Miss Trevisa's hand, turned his back on the house, and walked home snorting and muttering. On reaching Polzeath, however, he had cooled, and thought that possibly he had done a very foolish thing, and that most certainly he had in no way helped himself to what he desired, to see Judith again. Moreover, with a qualm, he became aware that

Oliver, on his return from Bristol, would in all probability greatly disapprove of this fiery outburst of temper. To what would it lead? *Could* he fight Captain Coppinger? If it came to that, he was ready. With all his faults Mr. Menaida was no coward.

On entering his house, he found Oliver there, just arrived from Camelford. He at once told him what he had done. Oliver did not reproach him; he merely said, "A declaration of war, father!—and a declaration before we are quite prepared."

"Well—I suppose so. I could not help myself. I was so incensed."

"The thing we have to consider," said Oliver, "is what Judith wishes, and how it is to be carried out. Some communication must be opened with her. If she desires to leave the house of that fellow, we must get her away. If, however, she elects to remain, our hands are tied: we can do nothing."

"It is very unfortunate that Jamie is no longer here; we could have sent her a letter through him."

"He has been removed to prevent anything of the sort taking place."

Then Oliver started up. " I will go and reconnoitre myself."

"No," said the father. "Leave all to me. You must on no account meddle in this matter ? "

" Why not ? "

"Because"—the old man coughed. " Do you not understand ?—you are a young man."

Oliver coloured, and said no more. He had not great confidence in his father's being able to do any-thing effectual for Judith. The step he had recently taken was injudicious and dangerous, and could further the end in view in no way.

He said no more to old Mr. Menaida, but he resolved to act himself in spite of the remonstrance made, and the objection raised by his father. No sooner was the elder man gone to bed, than he sallied forth and took the direction of Pentyre. It was a moonlight night. Clouds indeed rolled over the sky and for a while obscured the moon, but a moment after it flared forth again. A little snow had fallen and frosted the ground, making everything unburied by the white flakes to seem inky black. A cold wind whistled mournfully over the country. Oliver walked on, not feeling the cold, so glowing were his thoughts, and came within sight of the Glaze. His father had informed him that there were guests in the hall; but when he approached the house he could see no lights from the windows. Indeed the whole house was dark, as though every one in it were asleep, or it were an uninhabited ruin. That most of the windows had shutters he was aware, and that these might be shut so as to exclude the chance of any ray issuing he also knew. He could not therefore conclude that all the household had retired for the night. The moon was near its full. It hung high aloft in an almost cloudless sky. The air was comparatively still—still it never is on that coast, nor is it ever unthrilled by sound. Now, above the throb of the ocean, could be heard the shrill clatter and cry of the gulls. They were not asleep; they were about, fishing or quarrelling in the silver light.

Oliver rather wondered at the house being so hushed —wondered that the guests were all dismissed. He knew in which wing of the mansion was Judith's room, and also which was Judith's window. The pure white light shone on the face of the house and glittered in the window panes.

As Oliver looked, thinking and wondering, he saw
the casement opened, and Judith appeared at it, leaned
with her elbow on the sill, and rested her face in her
hand, looking up at the moon. The light air just lifted
her fine hair. Oliver noticed how delicately pale and
fragile she seemed—white as a gull, fragile as porcelain.
He would not disturb her for a moment or two; he
stood watching, with an oppression on his heart, and
with a film forming over his eyes. Could nothing be
done for the little creature? She was moped up in
her room. She was imprisoned in this house, and she
was wasting, dying in confinement.

And now he stole noiselessly nearer. There was an
old cattle-shed adjoining the house, that had lost its
roof. Coppinger concerned himself little about agri-
culture, and the shed that had once housed cows had
been suffered to fall to ruin, the slates had been blown
off, then the rain had wetted and rotted the rafters, and
finally the decayed rafters had fallen with their
remaining load of slates, leaving the walls alone
standing.

Up one of the sides of this ruinous shed Oliver
climbed, and then mounted to the gable, whence he

could speak to Judith. But she must have heard him, and been alarmed, for she hastily closed the casement. Oliver, however, did not abandon his purpose. He broke off particles of mortar from the gable of the cow-house, and threw them cautiously against the window. No notice was taken of the first or the second particle that clickered against a pane; but at the third a shadow appeared at the window, as though Judith had come to the casement to look out. Oliver was convinced that he could be seen, as he was on the very summit of the gable, and he raised his hands and arms to ensure attention. Suddenly the shadow was withdrawn. Then hastily he drew forth a scrap of paper, on which he had written a few words before he left his father's house, in the hopes of obtaining a chance of passing it to Judith, through Jamie, or by bribing a servant. This he now wrapped round a bit of stone and fastened it with a thread. Next moment the casement was opened and the shadow reappeared.

" Back ! " whispered Oliver, sufficiently loud to be heard, and he dexterously threw the stone and the letter through the open window.

Next moment the casement was shut, and the curtains were drawn.

He waited for full a quarter of an hour, but no answer was returned.

CHAPTER XLIII.

THE SECOND TIME.

No sooner had Oliver thrown the stone with note tied round it into Judith's room through the window, than he descended from a position which he esteemed too conspicuous should any one happen to be about in the night near the house. He ensconced himself beneath the cowshed wall in the shadow where concealed, but was ready, should the casement open, to step forth and show himself.

He had not been there many minutes before he heard steps and voices, one of which he immediately recognized as that of Cruel Coppinger. Oliver had not been sufficiently long in the neighbourhood to know the men in it by their voices, but, looking round the corner of the wall, he saw two figures against the horizon, one with hands in his pockets, and, by the general slouch, he thought that he recognized the sexton of St. Enodoc.

"The *Black Prince* will be in before long," said Coppinger. "I mean next week or fortnight, and I must have the goods shored here this time. She will stand off Porth-leze, and mind you get information conveyed to the captain of the coastguard that she will run her cargo there. Remember that. We must have a clear coast here. The stores are empty, and must be refilled."

"Yes, your honour."

"You have furnished him with the key to the signals?"

"Yes, Cap'n."

"And from Porth-leze there are to be signals to the *Black Prince* to come on here, but so that they may be read the other way—you understand?"

"Yes, Cap'n."

"And what do they give you every time you carry them a bit of information?"

"A shilling."

"A munificent Government payment! And what did they give you for the false code of signals?"

"Half a crown."

"Then here is half a guinea—and a crown for every lie you impose on them."

Then Coppinger and the sexton went further. As soon as Oliver thought he could escape unobserved, he withdrew and returned to Polzeath. Next day he had a talk with his father.

"I have had opinions, in Bristol," said he, "relative to the position of Judith."

"From whom?"

"From lawyers."

"Well—and what did they say?"

"One said one thing, and one another. I stated the case of her marriage, its incompletion, the unsigned register, and one opinion was that nevertheless she was Mrs. Coppinger. But another opinion was that, in consequence of the incompleteness of the marriage, it was none—she was Miss Trevisa. Father, before I went to the barristers and obtained their opinions, I was as wise as I am now, for I knew then what I know now, that she is either Mrs. Coppinger, or else that she is Miss Trevisa."

"I could have told you as much."

"It seems to me—but I may be uncharitable," said Oliver, grimly, "that the opinion given was this way or that way, according as I showed myself interested for the legality or against the legality of the marriage. Both of those to whom I applied regarded the case as interesting and deserving of being thrashed out in court of law, and gave their opinions so as to induce me to embark in a suit. You understand what I mean, father? When I seemed urgent that the marriage should be pronounced none at all, then the verdict of the consulting barrister was that it was no marriage at all, and very good reasons he was able to produce to show that. But when I let it be supposed that my object was to get this marriage established against certain parties keenly interested in disputing it, I got an opinion that it was a good and legal marriage, and very good reasons were produced to sustain this conclusion."

"I could have told you as much, and this has cost you money."

"Yes, naturally."

"And left you without any satisfaction."

"Yes."

"No satisfaction is to be got out of law—that is why I took to stuffing birds."

"What is that noise at the door?" asked Oliver.

"There is some one trying to come in, and fumbling at the hasp," said his father.

Oliver went to the door and opened it—to find Jamie there, trembling, white, and apparently about to faint. He could not speak, but he held out a ncte to Oliver.

"What is the matter with you?" asked the young man.

The boy, however, did not answer, but ran to Mr. Menaida and crouched behind him.

"He has been frightened," said the old man. "Leave him alone. He will come round presently, and I will give him a drop of spirits to rouse him up. What letter is that?"

Oliver looked at the little note given him. It had been sealed, but torn open afterwards. It was addressed to him, and across the address was written in bold, coarse letters, with a pencil, "Seen and passed.—C. C." Oliver opened the letter and read as follows :—

"I pray you leave me. Do not trouble yourself

about me. Nothing can now be done for me. My great concern is for Jamie. But I entreat you to be very cautious about yourself where you go. You are in danger. Your life is threatened, and you do not know it. I must not explain myself, but I warn you. Go out of the country—that would be best. Go back to Portugal. I shall not be at ease in my mind till I know that you are gone, and gone unhurt. My dear love to Mr. Menaida.—JUDITH."

The hand that had written this letter had shaken; the letters were hastily and imperfectly formed. Was this the hand of Judith who had taught Jamie callig- raphy, had written out his copies as neatly and beautifully as copper-plate?

Judith had sent him this answer by her brother, and Jamie had been stopped, forced to deliver up the missive, which Coppinger had opened and read. Oliver did not for a moment doubt *whence* the danger sprang with which he was menaced. Coppinger had suffered the warning to be conveyed to him with contemptuous indifference; it was as though he had scored across the letter, " Be forewarned, take what precautions you will, you shall not escape me."

The first challenge had come from old Menaida, but Coppinger passed over that as undeserving of attention; but he proclaimed his readiness to cross swords with the young man. And Oliver could not deny that he had given occasion for this. Without counting the cost, without considering the risk, nay, further, without weighing the right and wrong in the matter, Oliver had allowed himself to slip into terms of some familiarity with Judith, harmless enough, were she unmarried, but hardly calculated to be so regarded by a husband. They had come to consider each other as cousins, or they had pretended so to consider each other, so as to justify a half-affectionate, half-intimate association; and, before he was aware of it, Oliver had lost his heart. He could not, and he would not, regard Judith as the wife of Coppinger, because he knew that she absolutely refused to be so regarded by him, by herself, by his father, though by appearing at the ball with Coppinger, by living in his house, she allowed the world to so consider her. Was she his wife? He could not suppose it when she had refused to conclude the marriage ceremony, when there was no documentary evidence for the marriage. Let the question be mooted in a court of law. What could the witnesses say—but that she had fainted, and that all the latter portion of the ceremony had been performed over her when unconscious, and that on her recovery of her faculties she had resolutely persisted in resistance to the affixing of her signature to the register.

With respect to Judith's feelings towards himself, Oliver was ignorant. She had taken pleasure in his society because he had made himself agreeable to her, and his company was a relief to her after the solitude of Pentyre and the association there with persons with whom she was wholly out of sympathy?

His quarrel with Coppinger had shifted ground. At first he had resolved, should occasion offer, to conclude with him the contest begun on the wreck, and to chastise him for his conduct on that night. Now he thought little of that cause of resentment; he desired to punish him for having been the occasion of so much misery to Judith. He could not now drive from his head the scene of the girl's wan face at the window looking up at the moon.

Oliver would shrink from doing anything dishonourable, but it did not seem to him that there could be

aught wrong and unbecoming a gentleman in endeav-
ouring to snatch this hapless child from the claws of
the wild beast that had struck it down.

"No, father!" said he, hastily, as the old fellow
was pouring out a pretty strong dose of his great
specific and about to administer it to Jamie—"no,
father. It is not that the boy wants; and remember
how strongly Judith objects to his being given spirits."

"Dear! dear!" exclaimed Uncle Zachie, "to—be—
sure she does, and she made me promise not to give
him any. But this is an exceptional case."

"Let him come to me; I will soothe him. The
child is frightened; or, stay—get him to help you with
that kittiwake. Jamie! father can't get the bird to
look natural. His head does not seem to me to be
right. Did you ever see a kittiwake turn his neck in
that fashion? I wish you would put your fingers
to the throat and bend it about, and set the wadding
where it ought to be. Father and I can't agree about
it."

"It is wrong," said Jamie. "Look—this is the
way——"

His mind was diverted. Always volatile, always

ready to be turned from one thing to another, Oliver
had succeeded in interesting him, and had made him
forget for a moment the terrors that had shaken him.

After Jamie had been in the house for half an hour,
Oliver advised him to return to the Glaze. He would
give him no message, verbal or written. But the
thought of having to return renewed the poor child's
fears, and Oliver could hardly allay them by promising
to accompany him part of the way.

Oliver was careful not to speak to him on the subject
of his alarm, but he gathered from his disjointed talk
that Judith had given him the note, and impressed on
him that it was to be delivered as secretly as possible,
that Coppinger had intercepted him, and, suspecting
something, had threatened, frightened him into divulg-
ing the truth. Then Captain Cruel had read the letter,
scored over it some words in pencil, given it back to
him, and ordered him to fulfil his commission—to
deliver the note.

" Look you here, Jamie," was Mr. Menaida's parting
injunction to the lad as he left the house, "there's no
reason for you to be idle when at Pentyre. You can
make friends with some of the men, and get birds shot.

I don't advise your having a gun, you are not careful enough. But, if they shoot birds, you may amuse your leisure in skinning them, and I gave Judith arsenic for you. She keeps it in her workbox, and will let you have sufficient for your purpose, as you need it. I would not give it to you, as it might be dangerous in your hands as a gun. It is a deadly poison, and with carelessness you might kill a man. But go to Judith, when you have a skin ready to dress, and she will see that you have sufficient for the dressing. There, good-bye—and bring me some skins shortly."

Oliver accompanied the boy as far as the gate that led into the lane between the walls enclosing the fields of the Pentyre estate. Jamie pressed him to come further, but this the young man would not do. He bade the poor lad farewell, bid him divert himself, as his father had advised, with bird-stuffing, and remained at the gate watching him depart. The boy's face and feebleness touched and stirred the heart of Oliver. The face reminded him so strongly of his twin-sister, but it was the shadow, the pale shadow, of Judith only, without the intelligence, the character, and the force. And the helplessness of the child, his desolation, his condition of nervous alarm, roused the young man's pity. He was startled by a shot that struck his grey hat simultaneously with the report. In a moment he sprang over the hedge in the direction whence the smoke rose, and came upon Cruel Coppinger with a gun.

"Oh, you!" said the latter, with a sneer. "I thought I was shooting a rabbit."

"This is the second time," said Oliver.

"The first," was Coppinger's correction.

"Not so—the second time you have levelled at me. The first was on the wreck when I struck up your hand."

Coppinger shrugged his shoulders.

"It is immaterial. The third time is lucky, folks say."

The two men looked at each other with hostility.

"Your father has insulted me," said Coppinger. "Are you ready to take up his cause? I will not fight an old fool."

"I am ready to take up his cause, mine also, and that of——"

Oliver checked himself.

"And that of whom?" asked Coppinger, white with rage, and in a quivering voice.

" The cause of my father and mine own will suffice," said Oliver.

" And when shall we meet ? " asked Captain Cruel, leaning on his gun, and glaring at his young antagonist over it.

" When and where suits me," answered Oliver, coldly.

" And when and where may that be ? "

" When and where !—when and where I can come suddenly on you as you came on me upon the wreck. With such as you one does not observe the ordinary rules."

" Very well," shouted Coppinger. " When and where suits you, and when and where suits me—that is, whenever we meet again, we meet finally."

Then each turned and strode away.

CHAPTER XLIV.

THE WHIP FALLS.

FOR many days Judith had been as a prisoner in the house, in her room. Some one had spoken to Coppinger, and had roused his suspicions, excited his jealousy. He had forbidden her visits to Polzeath; and to prevent communication between her and the Menaida's, father and son, he had removed Jamie to Pentyre Glaze.

Angry and jealous he was. Time had passed, and still he had not advanced a step, rather he had lost ground. Judith's hopes that he was not what he had been represented were dashed. However plausible might be his story to account for the jewels, she did not believe it.

Why was Judith not submissive? Coppinger could

now only conclude that she had formed an attachment
for Oliver Menaida—for that young man whom she
singled out, greeted with a smile, and called by his
Christian name. He had heard of how she had made
daily visits to the house of the father, how Oliver had
been seen attending her home, and his heart foamed
with rage and jealousy.

She had no desire to go anywhere now that she was
forbidden to go to Polzeath, and when she knew that
she was watched. She would not descend to the hall
and mix with the company often assembled there, and
though she occasionally went there when Coppinger
was alone, took her knitting and sat by the fire, and
attempted to make conversation about ordinary matters,
yet his temper, his outbursts of rancour, his impatience
of every other topic save their relations to each other,
and his hatred of the Menaidas, made it intolerable for
her to be with him alone, and she desisted from seeking
the hall. This incensed him, and he occasionally went
upstairs, sought her out, and insisted on her coming
down. She would obey, but some outbreak would
speedily drive her from his presence again.

Their relations were more strained than ever. His

love for her had lost the complexion of love, and had assumed that of jealousy. His tenderness and gentleness towards her had been fed by hope, and when hope died they vanished. Even that reverence for her innocence, and the respect for her character that he had shown, were dissipated by the stormy gusts of jealousy.

Miss Trevisa was no more a help and stay to the poor girl than she had been previously. She was soured and embittered, for her ambition to be out of the house and in Othello Cottage had been frustrated. Coppinger would not let her go till he and his wife had come to more friendly terms.

On Judith's chimney-piece were two bunches of lavender, old bunches from the rectory garden of the preceding year. They had become so dry that the seeds fell out, and they no longer exhaled scent unless pressed.

Judith stood at her chimney-piece pressing her fingers on the dropped seeds, and picking them up by this means to throw them into the small fire that smouldered in the grate. At first she went on listlessly picking up a seed and casting it into the fire, actuated by her innate love of order, without much thought—rather

without any thought—for her mind was engaged over
the letter of Oliver, and his visit the previous night
outside. But after a while, whilst thus gathering the
grains of lavender, she came to associate them with
her trouble, and as she thought—Is there any escape
for me, any happiness in store ?—she picked up a seed
and cast it into the fire ; then she asked : Is there any
other escape for me than to die—to die and be with
dear papa again ; now not in S. Enodoc rectory
garden, but in the Garden of Paradise ? and again she
picked up and cast away a grain. Then, as she
touched her finger-tip with her tongue and applied it
to another lavender seed, she said : Or must this go
on—this nightmare of wretchedness, of persecution, of
weariness to death without dying—for years ? and she
cast away the seed shudderingly. Or—and again, now
without touching her finger with her tongue, as though
the last thought had contaminated it—or will he
finally break and subdue me, destroy me and Jamie,
soul and body ? Shivering at the thought, she hardly
dare to touch a seed, but forced herself to do so, raised
one and hastily shook it from her.

Thus she continued ringing the change, never for-

mulating any scheme of happiness for herself—certainly
in her white, guileless mind, not in any way associating
Oliver with happiness, save as one who might by some
means effect her discharge from this bondage, but he was
not linked, not woven up with any thought of the future.

The wind clickered at the casement. She had a
window towards the sea, another opposite, towards the
land.   Her's was a transparent chamber, and her mind
had been transparent.   Only now, timidly, doubtfully,
not knowing herself why, did she draw a blind down
over her soul, as though there were something there
that she would not have all the world see, and yet
which was in itself innocent.

Then a new fear woke up in her lest she should go
mad.   Day after day, night after night, was spent in
the same revolution of distressing thought, in the same
bringing up and reconsidering of old difficulties,
questions concerning Coppinger, questions concerning
Jamie, questions concerning her own power of endurance and resistance.   Was it possible that this
could go on without driving her mad ?

"One thing I see," murmured she ; "all steps are
broken away from under me on the stair, and one thing

alone remains for me to cling to—one only thing—my understanding. That"—she put her hands to her head, "that is all I have left. My name is gone from me, my friends I am separated from. My brother may not be with me. My happiness is all gone. My health may break down, but to a clear understanding I must hold, if that fails me I am lost—lost indeed."

"Lost indeed!" exclaimed Coppinger, entering abruptly.

He had caught her last words. He came in, in white rage, blinded and forgetful in his passion, and with his hat on. There was a day when he entered the rectory with his head covered, and Judith, without a word, by the mere force of her character shining out of her clear eyes, had made him retreat and uncover. It was not so now. She was careless whether he wore the hat or not when he entered her room.

"So!" said he, in a voice that foamed out of his mouth, "letters pass between you! Letters. I have read that you sent. I stayed your messenger."

"Well," answered Judith, with such composure as she could muster. She had already passed through several stormy scenes with him, and knew that her only security lay in self-restraint. "There was naught in it that you might not read. What did I say?—that my condition was fixed—that none could alter it. That is true. That my great care and sorrow of heart are for Jamie. That is true. That Oliver Menaida has been threatened. That also is true. I have heard you speak words against him of no good."

"I will make good my words."

"I wrote—and hoped to save him from a danger, and you from a crime."

Coppinger laughed.

"I have sent on the letter. Let him take what precautions he will. I will chastise him. No man ever crossed me yet but was brought to bite the dust."

"He has not harmed you, Captain Coppinger."

"He—! Can I endure that you should call him by his Christian name, whilst I am but Captain Coppinger? that you should seek him out, laugh and talk and flirt with him——"

"Captain Coppinger!"

"Yes," raged he, "always Captain Coppinger, or Captain Cruel, and he is dear Oliver! sweet Oliver!"

He well-nigh suffocated in his fury.

Judith drew herself up and folded her arms. She had in one hand a sprig of lavender, from which she had been shaking the over-ripe grains. She turned deadly white.

"Give me up his letter. Yours was an answer."

"I will give it to you," answered Judith, and she went to her workbox, raised the lid, then the little tray containing reels, and from beneath it extracted a crumpled scrap of paper. She handed it calmly, haughtily, to Coppinger, then folded her arms again, one hand still holding the bunch of lavender.

The letter was short. Coppinger's hand shook with passion so that he could hardly hold it with sufficient steadiness to read it. It ran as follows :—

"I must know your wishes, dear Judith. Do you intend to remain in that den of wreckers and cut-throats? or do you desire that your friends should bestir themselves to obtain your release? Tell us, in one word, what to do, or rather what are your wishes, and we will do what we can."

"Well," said Coppinger, looking up. "And your answer is to the point—you wish to stay."

" I did not answer thus.   I said, ' Leave me.' "

"And never intended that he should leave you," raged Coppinger.   He came close up to her with his eyes glittering, his nostrils distended and snorting, and his hands clenched.

Judith loosened her arms, and with her right hand swept a space before her with the bunch of lavender. He should not approach her within arm's length ; the lavender marked the limit beyond which he might not draw near.

" Now, hear me ! " said Coppinger.   " I have been too indulgent.   I have humoured you as a spoiled child.   Because you willed this or that I have sub-mitted.   But the time for humouring is over.   I can endure this suspense no longer.   Either you are my wife or you are not.   I will suffer no trifling over this any longer.   You have, as it were, put your lips to mine, and then sharply drawn them away, and now offer them to another."

" Silence ! " exclaimed Judith.   " You insult me."

" You insult and outrage me ! " said Coppinger, " when you run from your home to chatter with and walk with this Oliver, and never deign to speak to me.

When he is your dear Oliver, and I am only Captain Coppinger ; when you have smiles for him you have black looks for me. Is not that insulting, galling, stinging, maddening ? "

Judith was silent. Her throat swelled. There was some truth in what he said ; but, in the sight of heaven, she was guiltless of ever having thought of wrong, of having supposed for a moment that what she had allowed herself had not been harmless.

" You are silent," said Coppinger. " Now hearken ! With this moment I turn over the page of humouring your fancies and yielding to your follies. I have never pressed you to sign that register ; I have trusted to your good sense and good feeling. You cannot go back. Even if you desire it you cannot undo what has been done. Mine you are, mine you shall be—mine wholly and always. Do you hear ? "

" Yes."

" And agree ? "

" No."

He was silent a moment, with clenched teeth and hands, looking at her with eyes that smote her as though they were bullets.

"Very well," said he. "Your answer is ' No.' "

" My answer is No. So help me, God."

" Very well," said he, between his teeth. " Then we open a new chapter."

" What chapter is that ? "

" It is that of compulsion. That of solicitation is closed."

" You cannot, whilst I have my senses. What ! " She saw that he had a great riding-whip in his hand. " What — the old story again ? You will strike me ? "

" No, not you. I will lash you into submission— through Jamie."

She uttered a cry, dropped the lavender, that became scattered before her, and held up her hands in mute entreaty.

" I owe him chastisement. I have owed it him for many a day—and to day above all—as a go-between."

Judith could not speak. She remained as one frozen —in one attitude, in one spot, speechless. She could not stir, she could not utter a word of entreaty, as Coppinger left the room.

In another moment a loud and shrill cry reached her

ears from the court, into which one of her windows looked. She knew the cry. It was that of her twin-brother, and it thrilled through her heart, quivered in every nerve of her whole frame.

She could hear what followed ; but she could not stir. She was rooted by her feet to the floor ; but she writhed there. It was as though every blow dealt the boy out-side fell on her : she bent, she quivered ; her lips parted, but cry she could not, the sweat rolled off her brow, she beat with her hands in the air. Now she thrilled up, with uplifted arms, on tip-toe, then sank—it was like a flame flickering in a socket before it expires : it dances, it curls, it shoots up in a tongue, it sinks into a bead of light, it rolls on one side, it sways to the other, it leaps from the wick high into the air, and drops again. It was so with Judith—every stroke dealt, every scream of the tortured boy, every toss of his suffering frame, was repeated in her room, by her, in supreme, unspeaking anguish, too intense for sound to issue from her contracted throat.

Then all was still, and Judith had sunk to her knees on the scattered lavender, extending her arms, clasping her hands, spreading them again, again beating her palms together in a vague, unconscious way, as if in breathing she could not gain breath enough without this expansion and stretching forth of her arms.

But, all at once, before her stood Coppinger, the whip in his hands.

" Well, what now is your answer ? "

She breathed fast for some moments, labouring for expression. Then she reared herself up and tried to speak, but could not. Before her, thrashed out on the floor, were the lavender seeds. They lay thick in one place in a film over the boards. She put her finger among them and drew—NO.

CHAPTER XLV.

THERE are persons—they are not many—on whom Luck smiles and showers gold. Not a steady, daily, down-pour of money, but, whenever a little cloud darkens their sky, that same little cloud, which to others would be mere gloom, opens and discharges on them a sprinkling of gold pieces.

It is not always the case that those who have rich relatives come in for good things from them. In many cases there are such on whom Luck turns her back; but to those of whom we speak the rain of gold, and the snow of scrip and bonds, comes unexpectedly, but in-evitably. Just as Pilatus catches every cloud that drifts over Switzerland, so do they by some fatality catch something out of every trouble, that tends

materially to solace their feelings, lacerated by that
trouble. But not so only. These little showers fall
to them from relatives they have taken no trouble to
keep on good terms with, from acquaintances whom
they have cut, admirers whose good opinion they have
not concerned themselves to cultivate, friends with
whom they have quarrelled.

Gideon's fleece, on one occasion, gathered to itself
all the dew that fell, and left the grass of the field
around quite dry. So do these fortunate persons
concentrate on themselves, fortuitously it seems, the
dew of richness that descends and might have, ought
to have, dropped elsewhere, at all events, ought to have
been more evenly and impartially distributed. Gideon's
fleece, on another occasion, was dry, when all the glebe
was dripping. So is it with certain unfortunates—Luck
never favours them. What they have expected and
counted on they do not get, it is diverted, it drops
round about them on every side, only on them it never
falls.

Now, Miss Trevisa cannot be said to have belonged to
either of these classes. To the latter she had per-
tained, till suddenly, from a quarter quite unregarded,

there came down on her a very satisfactory little splash. Of relatives that were rich she had none, because she had no relatives at all. Of bosom friends she had none, for her bosom was of that unyielding nature, that no one would like to be taken to it. But, before the marriage of her brother, and before he became rector of S. Enodoc, when he was but a poor curate, she had been companion to a spinster lady, Miss Ceely, near S. Austell. Now, the companion is supposed to be a person without an opinion of her own, always standing in a cringing position to receive the opinion of her mistress, then to turn it over and give it forth as her own. She is, if she be a proper companion, a mere echo of the sentiments of her employer. Moreover, she is expected to be amiable, never to resent a rude word, never to take umbrage at neglect, always to be ready to dance attendance on her mistress, and with enthusiasm of devotion, real or simulated, to carry out her most absurd wishes, unreasoningly.

But Miss Trevisa had been, as a companion, all that a companion ought not to be. She had argued with Miss Ceely, invariably had crossed her opinions, had grumbled at her when she asked that anything might be done, raised difficulties, piled up objections, blocked the way to whatever Miss Ceely particularly set her heart on having executed. The two ladies were always quarrelling, always calling each other names, and it was a marvel to the relatives of Miss Ceely that she and her companion hung together for longer than a month. Nevertheless they did. Miss Trevisa left the old lady when Mr. Peter Trevisa became rector of S. Enodoc, and then Miss Ceely obtained in her place quite an ideal companion, a very mirror—she had but to look on her face, smile, and a smile was repeated, weep, and tears came in the mirror. The new companion grovelled at her feet, licked the dust off her shoes, fawned on her hand, ran herself off her legs to serve her, grew grey under the misery of enduring Miss Ceely's jibes and sneers and insults, finally sacrificed her health in nursing her. When Miss Ceely's will was opened it was found that she had left nothing, not a farthing, to this obsequious attendant, but had bequeathed fifteen hundred pounds, free of legacy duty, and all her furniture and her house to Miss Trevisa, with whom she had not kept up correspondence for twenty-three years. It really seemed as if leathery, rusty Aunt Dionysia,

from being a dry Gideon's fleece, were about to be
turned into a wet, wringable fleece. No one was
more astounded than herself.

It was now necessary that Miss Trevisa should go to
S. Austell, and see after what had come to her thus un-
solicited and unexpectedly. All need for her to remain
at Pentyre was at an end.

Before she departed—not finally, but to see about the
furniture that was now hers, and to make up her mind
whether to keep or to sell it—she called Judith to her.

That day, the events of which were given in last
chapter, had produced a profound impression on Jamie.
He had become gloomy, timid, and silent. His old idle
chatter ceased. He clung to his sister, and accompanied
her wherever she went ; he could not endure to be with
Coppinger ; when he heard his voice, caught a glimpse
of him, he ran away and hid. Jamie had been humoured
as a child, never beaten, scolded, put in a corner, sent
to bed, cut off his pudding ; but the rod had now been
applied to his back, and his first experience of corporal
punishment was the cruel and vindictive hiding ad-
ministered, not for any fault he had committed, but
because he had done his sister's bidding. He was

filled with hatred of Coppinger, mingled with fear, and when alone with Judith would break out into exclamations of entreaty that she would run away with him, and of detestation of the man who held them there, as it were, prisoners.

"Ju," said he, "I wish he were dead. I hate him! Why doesn't God kill him and set us free?"

At another time he said, "Ju, dear, you do not love him? I wish I were a big, strong man like Oliver, and I would do what Captain Cruel did."

"What do you mean?"

"Captain Cruel shot at Oliver."

This was the first tidings Judith had heard of the attempt on Oliver's life.

"He is a mean coward," said Jamie. "He hid behind a hedge and shot at him. But he did not hurt him."

"God preserved him," said Judith.

"Why does not God preserve us? Why did God let that beast——"

"Hush, Jamie!"

"I will not—that wretch beat me? Why did He not send lightning and strike him dead?"

"I cannot tell you, darling. We must wait and trust."

"I am tired of waiting and trusting. If I had a gun I would not shoot birds, I would go behind a hedge and shoot Captain Coppinger. There would be nothing wrong in that, Ju?"

"Yes, there would. It would be a sin."

"Not after he did that to Oliver."

"I would never, never love you if you did that."

"You would always love me, whatever I did," said Jamie.

He spoke the truth; Judith knew it. Her eyes filled she drew the boy to her, passionately, and kissed his golden head.

Then came Aunt Dionysia, and summoned her into her own room. Jamie followed.

"Judith," began Aunt Dunes, in her usual hard tones, and with the same frozen face, "I wish you particularly to understand. Look here! you have caused me annoyance enough whilst I have been here. Now I shall have a house of my own at S. Austell, and if I choose to live in it I can. If I do not, I can let it, and live at Othello Cottage. I have not made up my mind what to do. Fifteen hundred pounds is a dirty little sum, and not half as much as ought to have been left me for all I had to bear from that old woman. I am glad for one thing that she has left me something, though not much. I should have despaired of her salvation had she not. However, her heart was touched at the last, though not touched enough. Now, what I want you to understand is this—it entirely depends on your conduct, whether, after my death, this sum of fifteen hundred pounds, and a beggarly sum of about five hundred I have of my own, comes to you or not. As long as this nonsense goes on between you and Captain Coppinger—you pretending you are not married, when you are—there is no security for me that you and Jamie may not come tumbling in upon me, and become a burden to me. Captain Coppinger will not endure this fooling much longer. *He* can take advantage of your mistake. *He* can say : ' I am not married. Where is the evidence ? Produce proof of the marriage having been solemnized.' And then he may send you out of his house upon the downs in the cold. What would you be then, eh ? All the world holds you to be Mrs. Coppinger. A nice state of affairs if it wakes up one morning to hear that Mrs. Coppinger has been kicked out of the Glaze, that she never was the wife! What will the world say, eh? What sort of name will the world give you, when you have lived here as his wife?"

"That I have not."

"Lived here, gone to balls as his wife when you were not. What will the world call you, eh?"

Judith was silent, holding both her hands open against her bosom, Jamie beside her looking up in her face, not understanding what his aunt was saying.

"Very well—or rather, very ill," continued Miss Trevisa. "And then you and this boy here will come to me to take you in; come and saddle yourselves on me, and eat up my little fund. That is what will be the end of it, if you remain in your folly. Go at once to the rector, and put your name where it should have been two months ago, and your position is secure. He cannot drive you away, disgusted at your stubbornness, and you will relieve me of a constant source of uneasiness. It is not that only, but I must care for the good name of Trevisa, which you happen to bear, that that name may not be trailed in the dust. The common sense of the matter is precisely what you cannot see. If you are not Coppinger's wife, you should not be here. If you are Coppinger's wife, then your name should be in the register. Now, here you have come. You have appeared in public with him. You have but one course open to you, and that is to secure your position, and your name and honour. You cannot undo what is done, but you can complete what is done insufficiently. The choice between alternatives is no longer before you. If you had purposed to withdraw from marriage, break off the engagement, then you should not have come on to Pentyre and remained here. As, however, you did this, there is absolutely nothing else to be done but to sign the register. Do you hear me ? "

" Yes."

" And you will obey ? "

" No."

" Pig-headed fool ! " said Miss Trevisa ; " not one penny will I leave you, that I swear, if you remain obstinate."

" Do not let us say anything more about that, aunt. Now you are going away, is there anything connected

with the house you wish me to attend to. That I will
do, readily."

"Yes, there are several things," growled Miss Trevisa.
"And, first of all, are you disposed to do anything,
any common little kindness, for the man whose bread
you eat, whose roof covers you?"

"Yes, aunt."

"Very well, then. Captain Coppinger has his bowl
of porridge every morning. I suppose he was accustomed to it before he came into these parts, and
he cannot breakfast without it. He says that our
Cornish maids cannot make porridge properly, and I
have been accustomed to see to it. Either it is lumpy,
or it is watery, or it is saltless. Will you see to that?"

"Yes, aunt, willingly."

"You ought to know how to make porridge, as you
are more than half Scottish."

"I certainly can make it. Dear papa always liked
it."

"Then you will attend to that. If you are too high
and too great a lady to put your hand to it yourself,
you can see that the cook manages it aright. There is
a new girl in now, who is a fool."

" I will make it myself.   I will do all I can do."

" Then take the keys.   Now that I go, you must be mistress of the house.   But for your folly I might have been .rom here and in my own house, or rather in that given me for my use, Othello Cottage.   I was to have gone there directly after your marriage.   I had furnished it and made it comfortable, and then you took to your fantastic notions, and hung back, and refused to allow that you were married, and so I had to stick on here two months.   Here, take the keys."   Miss Trevisa almost flung them at her niece.   " Now I have two thousand pounds of my own, and a house at S. Austell, it does not become me to be doing menial service.   Take the keys.   I will never have them back."

When Miss Trevisa was gone, and Judith was by herself, at night, Jamie being asleep, she was able to think over calmly what her aunt had said.   She concerned herself not in the least relative to the promise her aunt had made of leaving her two thousand pounds were she submissive, and her threat of disinheriting her should she continue recalcitrant ; but she did feel that there was truth in her aunt's words when she said that she, Judith, had placed herself in a wrong position, but it was a wrong position into which she had been forced, she had not voluntarily entered it. She had, indeed, consented to become Coppinger's wife, but when she found that Coppinger had employed Jamie to give signals that might lead a vessel to its ruin, she could not go further to meet him. Although he had endeavoured to clear himself in her eyes, she did not believe him. She was convinced that he was guilty, though at moments she hoped, and tried to persuade herself, that he was not. Then came the matter of the diamonds. There again the gravest suspicion rested on him. Again he had endeavoured to exculpate himself, yet she could not believe that he was innocent. Till full confidence that he was blameless in these matters was restored, an insuperable wall divided them. Never would she belong to a man who was a wrecker, who belonged to that class of criminals her father had regarded with the utmost horror.

Before she retired to bed she picked up from under the fender the scrap of paper on which Oliver's message had been written. It had lain there unobserved where Coppinger had flung it. Now, as she tidied her room and arranged the fire rug, she observed it. She smoothed it out, folded it, and went to her workbox to replace it where it had been before.

She raised the lid, and was about to put the note among some other papers she had there—a letter of her mother's, a piece of her father's writing, some little accounts she had kept—when she was startled to see that the packet of arsenic Mr. Menaida had given her was missing.

She turned out the contents of her workbox. It was nowhere to be found, either there or in her drawers. Her aunt must have been prying into the box, have found and removed it, so Judith thought, and with this thought appeased her alarm. Perhaps, considering the danger of having arsenic about, Aunt Dionysia had done right in removing it. She had done wrong in doing so without speaking to Judith.

CHAPTER XLVI.

A SECOND LIE.

NEXT day, Miss Trevisa being gone, Judith had to attend to the work of the house. It was her manifest duty to do so. Hitherto she had shrunk from the responsibility, because she shrank from assuming a position in the house to which she refused to consider that she had a right. Judith was perfectly competent to manage an establishment; she had a clear head, a love of order, and a power of exacting obedience of servants without incessant reproof. Moreover, she had that faculty, possessed by few, of directing others in their work, so that each moved along his or her own line and fulfilled the allotted work with ease. She had managed her father's house, and managed it admirably. She knew that, as the King's Government must be carried on, so the routine of a household must be kept going. Judith had sufficient acquaintance also with servants to be aware that the wheel would stop or move spasmodically unless an authoritative hand were applied to it to keep it in even revolution. She knew also that whatever happened in a house—a birth, a death, a wedding, an uproar—the round of common duties must be discharged, the meals prepared, the bread baked, the milk skimmed, the beds made, the carpets swept, the furniture dusted, the windows opened, the blinds drawn down, the table laid, the silver and glass burnished. Nothing save a fire which gutted a house must interfere with all this routine. Miss Trevisa was one of those ladies who, in their own opinion, are condemned by Providence never to have good servants. A benign Providence sheds good domestics into every other house save that which she rules. She is born under a star which inexecrably sends the scum and dregs of servantdom under her sceptre. Miss Trevisa regarded a servant as a cat regards a mouse, a dog regards a fox, and a dolphin a flying-fish, as something to be run after, snapped at, clawed, leaped upon, worried perpetually. She was incapable

of believing that there could be any good in a servant,
that there was any other side to a domestic save a
seamy side. She could make no allowance for ignorance, for weakness, for lightheartedness. A servant,
in her eyes, must be a drudge, ever working, never
speaking, smiling, taking a hand off the duster, without a mind above flue and tea-leaves, and unable to soar
above a cobweb, with a temper perfect in endurance
of daily, hourly fault-finding, nagging, grumbling, a mind
unambitious also of commendation. Miss Trevisa held
that every servant that a malign Providence had sent
her was clumsy, insolent, slatternly, unmethodical,
idle, wasteful, a gossip, a gadabout, a liar, a thief,
was dainty, greedy, one of a cursed generation; and
when, in the Psalms, David launched out in denun-
ciation of the enemies of the Lord, Miss Trevisa, when
she heard or read these psalms, thought of servantdom.
Servants were referred to when David said, " Hide me
from the insurrection of the wicked doers, who have
wet their tongues like a sword, that they may privily
shoot at him that is perfect "—*i.e.*, Me, was Miss
Trevisa's comment. "They encourage themselves in
mischief: and commune among themselves how they

may lay snares, and say that no man shall see them."
"And how," said Miss Trevisa, "can men be so blind
as not to believe that the Bible is inspired when David
hits the character of servants off to the life!"

And not the Psalms only, but the Prophets were full
of servants' delinquencies. What were Tyre and Egypt
but figures of servantdom shadowed before. What else
did Isaiah lift up his testimony about, and Jeremiah
lament over, but the iniquities of the kitchen and the
servants' hall. Miss Trevisa read her Bible, and great
comfort did it afford her, because it did denounce the
servant maids so unsparingly, and prepared brimstone
and outer darkness for them.

Now, Judith had seen and heard much of the way
in which Miss Trevisa managed Captain Coppinger's
house. Her room adjoined that of her aunt, and she
knew that if her aunt were engaged on—it mattered
not what absorbing work—embroidery, . darning a
stocking, reading a novel, saying her prayers, study-
ing the cookery book—if a servant sneezed within a
hundred yards, or upset a drop of water, or clanked
a dust-pan, or clicked a door-handle, Miss Trevisa
would be distracted from her work and rush out of

her room, just as a spider darts from its recess, and would sweep down on the luckless servant to worry and abuse her.

Judith, knowing this, knew also that the day of Miss Trevisa's departure would be marked with white chalk, and lead to a general relaxation of discipline, to an inhaling of long breaths, and a general stretching, and taking of ease. It was necessary, therefore, that she should go round and see that the wheel was kept turning. To her surprise, on entering the hall, she found Captain Coppinger there.

" I beg your pardon," she said, " I thought you were out."

She looked at him, and was struck with his appearance, the clay-like colour of his face, the dark lines in it, the faded look in his eyes.

" Are you unwell ? " she asked. " You really look ill."

" I am ill."

" Ill—what is the matter ? "

" A burning in my throat. Cramps and pains—but what is that to you ? "

" When did it come on ? "

" But recently."

" Will you not have a doctor to see you ? "

" A doctor !—no."

" Was the porridge as you liked it this morning ? I made it."

" It was good enough."

" Would you like more now ? "

" No."

" And to - morrow morning, will you have the same ? "

" Yes—the same."

" I will make it again. Aunt said the new cook did not understand how to mix and boil it to your liking."

Coppinger nodded.

Judith remained standing and observing him. Some faces when touched by pain and sickness are softened and sweetened. The hand of suffering passes over the countenance, and brushes away all that is frivolous, sordid, vulgar; it gives dignity, purity, refinement, and shows what the inner soul might be were it not entangled and degraded by base association and pursuit. It is different with other faces, the hand of suffering films away the assumed expression of good nature, honesty, straightforwardness, and unmasks the evil inner man. The touch of pain had not improved the expression of Cruel Coppinger. It cannot, however, with justice be said that the gentler aspect of the man which Judith had at one time seen was an assumption. He was a man in whom there was a certain element of good, but it was mixed up with headlong wilfulness, utter selfishness and resolution to have his own way at any cost.

Judith could see now that his face was pain-struck, how much of evil there was in the soul, that had been disguised by a certain dash of masculine over-bearing, and brusqueness.

"What are you looking at?" asked Coppinger, glancing up.

"I was thinking," answered Judith.

"Of what?"

"Of you—of Wyvill, of the wreck on Doom Bar, of the jewels of Lady Knighton, and, last of all, of Jamie's maltreatment."

"And what of all that?" he said, in irritable scorn.

"That I need not say. I have drawn my own conclusions."

"You torment me, you— when I am ill ? They call me cruel, but it is you who are cruel."

Judith did not wish to be drawn into discussion that. must be fruitless. She said quietly, in altered tone, " Can I get you anything to comfort you ? "

" No—go your way. This will pass. Besides, it is naught to you. Go ; I would be left alone."

Judith obeyed, but she was uneasy. She had never seen Coppinger look as he looked now. It was other altogether after he had broken his arm. Other also when for a day he was crippled with bruises after the wreck. She looked into the hall several times during the day. In the afternoon he was easier, and went out ; his mouth had been parched and burning, and he had been drinking milk. The empty glass was on the table. He would eat nothing at mid-day. He turned from food, and left the room for his own chamber.

Judith was anxious. She more than once endeavoured to draw Coppinger into conversation relative to himself, but he would not speak of what afflicted him. He was annoyed and ashamed at being out of his usual rude health. " It is naught," he said, " but a bilious attack, and will pass. Leave me alone."

She had been so busy all day that she had seen little of Jamie. He had taken advantage of Captain Coppinger not being about to give himself more licence to roam than he had of late, and to go with his donkey on the cliffs. Anyhow, Judith on this day did not have him hanging to her skirts. She was glad of it, for, though she loved him, he would have been an incumbrance when she was so busy.

The last thing at night she did was to go to Coppinger to inquire what he would take. He desired nothing but spirits and milk. He thought that a milk-punch would give him ease and make him sleep. That he was weak and had suffered pain she saw, and she was full of pity for him. But this she did not like to exhibit, partly because he might misunderstand her feelings, and partly because he seemed irritated at being unwell, and at loss of power; irritated at all events, at it being observed that he was not in his usual plenitude of strength and health.

That night the Atlantic was troubled, and the wind carried the billows against the cliffs in a succession of rhythmic roars that filled the air with sound, and made the earth quiver. Judith could not sleep; she listened to the thud of the water-heaps flung against the rocks. There was a clock on the stairs, and in her wakefulness she listened to the tick of the clock and the boom of the waves, now coming together, then one behind the other, now the wave-beat catching up the clock-tick, then falling in arrear, the ocean getting angry and making up its pace by a double beat. Moreover, flakes of foam were carried on the wind, and came like snow against her window that looked seaward, striking the glass, and adhering to it.

As Judith lay watchful in the night her mind again recurred to the packet of arsenic that had been abstracted from her workbox. It was inconsiderate of her to have left it there : she ought to have locked her box. But who could have supposed that any one would have gone to the box, raised the tray, and searched the contents of the compartment beneath ? Judith had been unaccustomed to lock up anything, because she had never had any secrets to hide from any eye. She again considered the probability of her aunt having removed it, and then it occurred to her that perhaps Miss Trevisa might have supposed that she, Judith, in a fit of revolt against the wretchedness

of her life, might be induced to take the poison herself
and finish her miseries. " It was absurd if Aunt Dunes
thought that," said Judith to herself; " she can little
have known how my dear papa's teaching has sunk
into my heart to suppose me capable of such a thing,
and then to run away like a coward, and leave Jamie
unprotected. It was too absurd."

Next morning Judith was in her room getting a large
needle with which to hem a bit of carpet-edge that had
been fraying for the last five years, and which no one
had thought of putting a thread to, and so arresting
the disintegration. Jamie was in the room. Judith
said to him :—

" My dear, you have not been skinning and stuffing
any birds lately, have you ? "

" No, Ju."

" Because I have missed—but, Jamie, I hope you
have not been at my workbox ? "

" What about your workbox, Ju ? "

She knew the boy so well that her suspicions were at
once aroused by this answer. When he had nothing
to hide he replied with a direct negative or affirmative,
but when he had done what his conscience would not

quite allow was right, he fell into equivocation and shuffled awkwardly.

"Jamie," said Judith, looking him straight in the face, "have you been to my box?"

"Only just looked in."

Then he ran to the window. "Oh, do see, Ju! how patched the glass is with foam!—and is it not dirty?"

"Jamie, come back! I want an answer."

He had opened the casement and put his hand out, and was wiping off the patches of froth.

"What a lot of it there is, Ju!"

"Come here instantly, Jamie, and shut the window."

The boy obeyed, creeping towards her sideways, with his head down.

"Jamie, did you lift the tray?"

"Only on one side, just a little bit."

"Did you take anything from under the tray?"

He did not answer immediately. She looked at him searchingly and in suspense. He never could endure this questioning look of hers, and he ran to her, put his arms round her waist, and, clasped to her side, hid his face in her gown.

"Only a little."

" A little what ? "

" I don't know."

" Jamie, no lies. There was a blue paper there containing poison that you were not to have unless there were occasion for it—some bird-skin to be preserved and dressed with it. Now—did you take that ? "

" Yes."

" Go and bring it back to me immediately."

" I can't."

" Why not ? Where is it ? "

The boy fidgeted, looked up in his sister's face to see what expression it bore, buried his head again, and said—

" Ju, he is rightly called Cruel. I hate him, and so do you—don't you, Ju ? I have put the arsenic into his oatmeal, and we will get rid of him and be free and go away—it will be jolly ! "

" Jamie ! " with a cry of horror.

" He won't whip me and scold you any more."

" Jamie ! Oh, my Lord, have pity on him ! Have pity on us ! "

She clasped her hands to her head, rushed from the room, and flew down the stairs.

But ten minutes before that Judith had given Coppinger his bowl of porridge. He had risen late that morning. He was better, he said, and he looked more himself than the preceding day. He was now seated at the table in the hall, and had poured the fresh milk into the bowl, had dipped the spoon, put some of the porridge to his mouth, tasted, and was looking curiously into the spoon, when the door was flung open, Judith entered, and without a word of explanation, caught the bowl from him and dashed it on the floor.

Coppinger looked at her with his boring dark eyes, intently, and said, " What is the meaning of this ? "

" It is poisoned."

Judith was breathless. She drew back, relieved at having cast away the fatal mess.

Coppinger rose to his feet and glared at her across the table, leaning with his knuckles on the board. He did not speak for a moment, his face became livid, and his hands resting on the table shook as though he were shivering in an ague.

" There is arsenic in the porridge," gasped Judith.

She had not had time to weigh what she should say,

how explain her conduct ; but one thought had held her
—to save Coppinger's life whilst there was yet time.

The Captain's dog, that had been lying at his
master's feet, rose, went to the spilt porridge, and
began to lap the milk and devour the paste. Neither
Judith nor Coppinger regarded him.

"It was an accident !" faltered Judith.

"You lie !" said Coppinger, in thrilling tones.
"You lie—you murderess ! You sought to kill me."

Judith did not answer for a moment. She also was
trembling. She had to resolve what course to pursue.
She could not, she would not, betray her brother, and
subject him to the worst brutality of treatment from the
infuriated man whose life he had sought.

It were better for her to take the blame on herself.

"I made the porridge—I and no one else."

"You told me so yesterday." He maintained his
composure marvellously, but he was stunned by the
sudden discovery of treachery in the woman he had
loved and worshipped.

"You maddened me by your treatment ; but I did
not desire that you should die. I repented and have
saved your life."

As Judith spoke she felt as though the flesh of her face stiffened, and the skin became as parchment. She could hardly open her mouth to speak and stir her tongue.

" Go!" said Coppinger, pointing to the door. "Go, you and your brother. Othello Cottage is empty. Go, murderess, poisoner of your husband, there, and wait till you hear from me. Under one roof, to eat off one board, is henceforth impossible. Go!" He remained pointing, and a sulphurous fire flickered in his eyes.

Then the hound began to howl, threw itself down, its limbs were contracted, it foamed at the mouth, and howled again.

To the howlings of the poisoned and dying dog Judith and Jamie left Pentyre.

CHAPTER XLVII.

FAST IN HIS HANDS.

JUDITH and Jamie were together in Othello Cottage—banished from Pentyre with a dark and threatening shadow over them, this however gave the boy but little concern; he was delighted to be away from a house where he had been in incessant terror, and where he was under restraint; moreover, it was joy to him to be now where he need not meet Coppinger at every turn.

Judith forbade his going to Polzeath to see Uncle Zachie and Oliver Menaida, as she thought it advisable under the circumstances to keep themselves to themselves, and, above all, not to give further occasion for the suspicions and jealousy of Coppinger. This was to her, under the present condition of affairs, specially distressing, as she needed some counsel as to what she should do. Uncle Zachie at his best was a poor adviser, but on no account now would she appeal to his son. She was embarrassed and alarmed, and she had excuse for embarrassment and alarm. She had taken upon herself the attempt that had been made on the life of Coppinger, and he would, she supposed, believe her to be guilty.

What would he do? Would he proceed against her for attempted murder? If so the case against her was very complete. It could be shown that Mr. Menaida had given her this arsenic, that she had kept it by her in her workbox whilst at the Glaze, that she had been on the most unsatisfactory terms with Captain Coppinger, and that she had refused to complete her marriage with him by appending her signature to the register. She was now aware—and the thought made her feel sick at heart and faint—that her association with the Menaidas had been most injudicious, and had been capable of misinterpretation. It had been misinterpreted by Coppinger, and probably also by the gossips of Polzeath. It could be shown that a secret correspondence had been carried on between her and Oliver, which had been intercepted by her husband.

This was followed immediately by the attempt to poison Coppinger. The arsenic had been given him in the porridge her own hands had mixed, and which had been touched by no one else. It was natural to conclude that she had deliberately purposed to destroy her husband that she might be free to marry Oliver Menaida.

If she were prosecuted on the criminal charge of attempted murder, the case could be made so conclusive against her that her conviction was certain.

Her only chances of escape lay in two directions— one, that she should tell the truth, and allow Jamie to suffer the consequences of what he had done, which would be prison or a lunatic asylum; the other was that she should continue to screen him and trust that Coppinger would not prosecute her. He might hesitate about proceeding with such a case, which would attract attention to himself, to his household, and lay bare to the public eye much that he would reasonably be supposed to wish to keep concealed. If, for instance, the case were brought into court, the story of the enforced marriage must come out, and that would rake up once more the mystery of the wreckers on

Doom Bar, and of Lady Knighton's jewels. Coppinger might, and probably would, grasp at the other alternative; take advantage of the incompletion of the marriage, repudiate her, and let the matter of the poisoned porridge remain untouched.

The more Judith turned the matter over in her head the more sure she became that the best course, indeed the only one in which safety lay, was for her to continue to assume to herself the guilt of the attempt on Coppinger's life. He would see by her interference the second time, and prevention of his taking a second portion of the arsenic, that she did not really seek his life, but sought to force him through personal fear to drive her from his house, and break the bond by which he bound her to him. For the sake of this going back from a purpose of murder, or because he thought that she had never intended to do more than drive him to a separation by alarm for his own safety; for the sake of the old love he had borne her, he might forbear pressing this matter to its bitter consequences, and accept what she desired—their separation.

But if Judith allowed the truth to come out, then her husband would have no such compunction. It would be an opportunity for him to get rid of the boy he detested, and even if he did not have him consigned to gaol, then it would be only because he would send him to an asylum.

Judith went out on the cliffs. The sea was troubled far as the horizon, strewn with white horses shaking their manes, pawing and prancing in their gallop landward. There was no blue, no greenness in the ocean now. The dull tinctures of winter were in it. The Atlantic wore its scowl, was leaden, and impatient. The foam on the rocks was driven up in spouts into the air and carried over the downs, it caught in the thorn-bushes like flocks of wool, and was no cleaner. It lay with the thin, melting snow, and melted with it into a dirty slush. It plastered the face of Othello Cottage, as though in brutal insolence Ocean had been spitting at the house that was built of the wreck he had failed to gulp down, though he had chewed the life out of it. The foam rested in flakes on the rushes, where it hung and fluttered like tufts of cotton grass. It was dropped about by the wind for miles inland, as though the wind were running in a paper-chase. It was as though sky and sea were contending in a game of pelting the land, the one with snow, the other with foam, the one sweet, the other salt. Judith walked near the edge of the cliffs, where there was no snow, and looked out at the angry ocean. All without was cold, rugged, ruffled, wretched; and within her heart burned a fire of apprehension, distress, almost of despair.

All at once she came upon Mr. Desiderius Mules, walking in an opposite direction, engaged in wiping the foam flakes out of his eyes.

"Halloa! you here, Mrs. Coppinger!" exclaimed the rector. "Glad to see you. I'm not here, like S. Anthony, preaching to the fishes, because I am a practical man. In the first place, in such a disturbed sea the fishes would have enough to do to look after themselves, and would be ill-disposed to lend me an ear. In the next place, the wind is on shore, and they could not hear me were I to lift up my voice. So I don't waste words and overstrain my larynx. If the bishop were a mile, or a mile-and-a-half, inland, it might be different; he might admire my zeal. And what brings you here?"

"Oh, Mr. Mules!" exclaimed Judith, with a leap of hope in her heart—here was some one who might, if he would, be a help to her. She had indeed made up her own mind as to what was the safest road on which to set her feet, but she was timid, shrank from false-hood, and earnestly craved for some one to whom she could speak, and from whom she could obtain advice.

" Oh, Mr. Mules ! will you give me some advice and assistance ? "

" Advice by all means," said the rector. " I'll turn and walk your way; the froth is blown into my face and stings it. My skin is sensitive, so are my eyes. Upon my word, when I get home my face will be as salt as if I had flooded it with tears. Fancy me crying. What did you say you wanted—advice ? "

" Advice and assistance."

" Advice you shall have, it is my profession to give it. I mix it with pepper and salt and serve it out in soup-plates every week—am ready with it every day, Mrs. Coppinger. I have buckets of it at your disposal, bring your tureen and I'll tip in as much of the broth as you want, and may you like it. As to assistance, that is another matter. Pecuniary assistance I never give. I am unable to do so. My principles stand in the way. I have set up a high standard for myself and I stick to it. I never render pecuniary assistance to any one, as it demoralizes the receiver. I hope and trust it was not pecuniary assistance you wanted."

" No, Mr. Mules; not that, only guidance."

" Oh, guidance! I'm your sign-post; where do you want to go ? "

" It is this, sir. I have given poison to Mr. Coppinger."

" Mercy on me ! "

The rector jumped back, and turned much the tinge of the foam plasters that were on his face.

" That is to say, I gave him arsenic mixed with his porridge the day before yesterday, and it made him very ill. Yesterday——"

" Hush, hush ! " said Mr. Mules, " no more of this. This is ghastly. Let us say it is hallucination on your part. You are either not right in your head or are very wicked. If you please, don't come nearer to me. I can hear you quite well, hear a great deal more than pleases me. You ask my advice, and I give it : Sign the register, that will set me square, and put me in an unassailable position with the public, and also, secondarily, it will be to your advantage. You are now a nondescript, and a nondescript is objectionable. If you please—you will excuse me—I should prefer *not* standing between you and the cliff. There is no knowing what a person who confesses to poisoning her husband might do. If it be a case of lunacy—well, more reason that I should use precautions. My life is valuable. Come, there is only one thing you can do to make me comfortable, sign the register."

"You will not mention what I have told you to any one ? "

"Save and defend us! I speak of it—I! Come, come, be rational. Sign the register and set my mind at ease. That is all I want and ask for, and then I wash my hands of you."

Then away went Mr. Desiderius Mules, with the wind catching his coat-tails, twisting them, throwing them up against his back, parting them, and driving them one on each side of them, taking and curling them and sending them between his legs.

Judith stood mournfully looking after him. The sign-post, as he had called himself, was flying from the traveller whom it was his duty to direct.

Then a hand was laid on her arm. She started,

turned and saw Oliver Menaida, flushed with rapid walking and with the fresh air he had encountered.

" I have come to see you," he said, " come to offer my father's and my assistance. We have just heard——"

" What ? "

" That Captain Coppinger has turned you and Jamie out of his house."

" Have you heard any reason assigned ? "

" Because—so it is said—he had beaten the boy, and you were incensed, angry words passed, and it ended in a rupture."

" That, then, is the common explanation."

" Every one is talking about it. Every one says that. And now, what will you do ? "

" Thank you. Jamie and I are at Othello Cottage, where we are comfortable. My aunt had furnished it intending to reside in it herself. As for our food, we receive that from the Glaze."

" But this cannot continue."

" It must continue for a while."

" And then ? "

" The future is not open to my eyes."

" Judith, that has taken place at length which I have been long expecting."

" What do you mean ? "

" This miserable condition of affairs has reached its climax, and there has been a turn."

Judith sighed. " It has taken a turn indeed."

" Now Captain Coppinger has been brought to his senses, and he sees that your resolve is not to be shaken, and he releases you, or you have released yourself from the thraldom you have been in. I do not suppose the popular account of the matter is true wholly."

" It is not at all true."

" That matters not. The fact remains that you are out of Pentyre Glaze and your own mistress. The snare is broken and you are delivered."

Again Judith sighed, and she shook her head despondingly.

" You are free," persisted Oliver. " Just consider. You were hurried through a marriage when insensible, and when you came to consciousness you did what was the only thing you could do—you absolutely refused your signature that would validate what had taken place. That was conclusive. That ceremony was as worthless as this sea-foam that blows by. No court in the world would hold that you were bound by it. The consent, the free consent, of each party in such a convention is essential. As to your being at Pentyre, nothing against that can be alleged; Miss Trevisa was your aunt, and constituted your guardian by your father. Your place was by her. To her you went when my father's house was no longer at your service through my return. At Pentyre you remained as long as Miss Trevisa was there. She went, and at once you left the house."

" You do not understand."

" Excuse me, I think I do. But no matter as to details. When your aunt went, you went also—as was proper under the circumstances. We have heard, I do not know whether it be true, that your aunt has come in for a good property."

" For a little something."

" Then shall you go to her and reside with her ? "

" No; she will not have Jamie and me."

" So we supposed. Now, my father has a proposal to make. The firm to which I belong has been good enough to take me into partnership, esteeming my services far higher than they deserve, and I am to live at Oporto and act for them there. As my income will now be far larger than my humble requirements, I have resolved to allow my dear father sufficient for him to live upon comfortably where he wills, and he has elected to follow me and take up his abode in Portugal. Now, what he has commissioned me to say is—Will you go with him? Will you continue to regard him as Uncle Zachie, and be to him as his dear little niece, and keep house for him in the sunny southern land?"

Judith's eyes filled with tears.

"And Jamie is included in the invitation. He is to come also, and help my father to stuff the birds of Portugal. A new ornithological field is opening before him, he says, and he must have help in it."

"I cannot," said Judith, in a low tone, with her head sunk on her breast. "I cannot leave here till Captain Coppinger gives me leave."

"But, surely, you are no longer bound to him?"

"He holds me faster than before."

"I cannot understand this."

"No; because you do not know all."

"Tell me the whole truth. Let me help you. Let

my father help you. You little know how we both
have our hearts in your service."

" Well, I will tell you."

But she hesitated and trembled. She fixed her eyes
on the wild, foaming, leaden sea, and pressed her bosom
with both hands.

" I poisoned him."

" Judith ! "

" It is true. I gave him arsenic, once ; that your
father had let me have for Jamie. If he had taken it
the second time, when I offered it him in his bowl of
porridge, he would be dead now. Do you see—he
holds me in his hands, and I cannot stir. I could not
escape till I know what he intends to do with me. Now
go—leave me to my fate."

" Judith—it is not true! Though I hear this from
your lips, I will not believe it. No ; you need my
father's, you need my help more than ever." He put
her hand to his lips. " It is white—innocent. I *know*
it, in spite of your words."

CHAPTER XLVIII.

TWO ALTERNATIVES.

WHEN Judith returned to Othello Cottage, she was surprised to see a man promenading around it, flattening his nose at the window, so as to bring his eyes against the glass, then, finding that the breath from his nostrils dimmed the pane, wiping the glass and again flattening his nose. At first he held his hands on the window ledge, but being incommoded by the refraction of the light, put the open hands against the pane, one on each side of his face. Having satisfied himself at one casement, he went to another, and made the same desperate efforts to see in at that.

Judith coming up to the door, and putting the key in, disturbed him. He started, turned, and with a nose much like putty, but rapidly purpling with returned circulation, disclosed the features of Mr. Scantlebray senior.

"Ah, ha!" said that gentleman, in no way disconcerted; "here I have you, after having been looking for my orphing charmer in every direction but the right one. With your favour I will come inside and have a chat."

"Excuse me," said Judith, "but I do not desire to admit visitors."

"But I am an exception. I'm the man who should have looked after your interests, and would have done it a deal better than others. And so there has been a rumpus, eh? What about?"

"I really beg your pardon, Mr. Scantlebray, but I am engaged and cannot ask you to enter, nor delay conversing with you on the doorstep."

"Oh, Jimminy! don't consider me. I'll stand on the doorstep and talk with you inside. Don't consider me; go on with what you have to do, and let me amuse you. It must be dull and solitary here, but I will enliven you, though I have not my brother's gifts. Now, Obadiah is a man with a genius for entertaining people. He missed his way when he started in life;

he would have made a comic actor. Bless your simple heart, had that man appeared on the boards he would have brought the house down."

"I have no doubt whatever he missed his way when he took to keeping an asylum," said Judith.

"We have all our gifts," said Scantlebray. "Mine is architecture; and 'pon my honour as a gentleman, I do admire the structure of Othello Cottage, uncommon. You won't object to my pulling out my tape and taking the plan of the edifice, will you?"

"The house belongs to Captain Coppinger; consult him."

"My dear orphing, not a bit. I'm not on the best terms with that gent. There lies a tract of ruffled water between us. Not that I have given him cause for offence, but that he is not sweet upon me. He took off my hands the management of your affairs in the valuation business, and let me tell you—between me and you and that post yonder—" he walked in and laid his hand on a beam—" that he mismanaged it confoundedly. He is your husband, I am well aware, and I ought not to say this to you. He took the job into his hands because he had an eye to you, I knew that well enough. But

he hadn't the gift—the faculty. Now I have made
all that sort of thing my speciality. How many rooms
have you in this house ? What does that door lead to ? '

" Really, Mr. Scantlebray, you must excuse me ; I
am busy."

" Oh, yes—vastly busy. Walking on the cliffs, eh ?
Alone, eh ? Well, ' mum ' is the word. Come, make
me your friend, and tell me all about it. How came
you here ? There are all kinds of stories afloat about
the quarrel between you and your husband, and he is
an Eolus, a blustering Boreas, all the winds in one box.
Not surprised. He blew up a gale against me once.
Domestic felicity is a fable of the poets. Home is a
region of cyclones, tornadoes, hurricanes—what you like
—anything but a Pacific Ocean. Now, you won't mind
my throwing an eye round this house, will you ? A
scientific eye. Architecture is my passion."

" Mr. Scantlebray, that is my bedroom ; I forbid your
touching the handle. Excuse me—but I must request
you to leave me in peace."

" My dear creature," said Scantlebray, " scientific
thirst before all. It is unslakable save by the acquisition of what it desires. The structure of this house, as

well as its object, has always been a puzzle to me. So your aunt was to have lived here—the divine, the fascinating Dionysia, as I remember her years ago. It wasn't built for the lovely Dionysia, was it? No. Then for what object was it built? And why so long untenanted? These are nuts for you to crack?"

"I do not trouble myself about these questions. I must pray you to depart."

"In half the twinkle of an eye," said Scantlebray. Then he seated himself. "Come, you haven't a superabundance of friends; make me one, and unburden your soul to me. What is it all about? Why are you here? What has caused this squabble? I have a brother a solicitor at Bodmin. Let me dot down the items, and we'll get a case out of it. Trust me as a friend, and I'll have you righted. I hear Miss Trevisa has come in for a fortune. Be a good girl, set your back against her and show fight."

"I will thank you to leave the house," said Judith, haughtily. "A moment ago you made reference to your honour as a gentleman. I must appeal to that same honour which you pride yourself on possessing, and by virtue of that request you to depart."

"I'll go, I'll go. But, my dear child, why are you in such a hurry to get rid of me? Are you expecting some one? It is an odd thing, but as I came along I was overtaken by Mr. Oliver Menaida, making his way to the downs—to look at the sea, which is rough, and inhale the breeze of the ocean, of course. At one time, I am informed, you made daily visits to Polzeath, daily visits whilst Captain Coppinger was on the sea; since his return, I am informed, these visits have been discontinued. Is it possible that, instead of your visiting Mr. Oliver, Mr. Oliver is now visiting you—here, in this cottage."

A sudden slash across the back and shoulders made Mr. Scantlebray jump and bound aside. Coppinger had entered, and was armed with a stout walking-stick.

"What brings you here?" he asked.

"I came to pay my respects to the grass widow," sneered Scantlebray, as he sidled to the door and bolted, but not till, with a face full of malignity, he had shaken his fist at Coppinger behind his back.

"What brings this man here?" asked the Captain.

"Impertinence—nothing else," answered Judith.

"What was that he said about Oliver Menaida?"

"His insolence will not bear reporting."

"You are right. He is a cur, and deserves to be kicked, not spoken to or spoken of. I heed him not. There is in him a grudge against me. He thought at one time that I would have taken his daughter. Do you recall speaking to me once about the girl that you supposed was a fit mate for me? I laughed. I thought you had heard the chatter about Polly Scantlebray and me. A bold, fine girl, full of blood as a cherry is full of juice—one of the stock, but with better looks than the men, yet with the assurance, the effrontery, of her father. A girl to laugh and talk with, not to take to one's heart. I care for Polly Scantlebray! Not I! That man has never forgiven me the disappointment because I did not take her. I never intended to. I despised her. Now you know all. Now you see why he hates me. I do not care. I am his match. But I will not have him insolent to you. What did he say?"

It was a relief to Judith that Captain Coppinger had not heard the words that Mr. Scantlebray had used. They would have inflamed his jealousy and fired him into fury against the speaker.

"He told me that he had been passed on his way hither by Mr. Oliver Menaida coming to the cliffs to inhale the sea air and look at the angry ocean."

Captain Coppinger was satisfied, or pretended to be so. He went to the door and shut it, but not till he had gone outside and looked round to see—so Judith thought—whether Oliver Menaida were coming that way quite as much as to satisfy himself that Mr. Scantlebray was not lurking round a corner listening.

No! Oliver Menaida would not come there. Of that Judith was quite sure. He had the delicacy of mind and the good sense not to risk her reputation by approaching Othello Cottage. When he had made that offer to her she had known that his own heart spoke, but he had veiled its speech, and had made the offer as from his father, and in such a way as not to offend her. Only when she had accused herself of attempted murder did he break through his reserve, to show her his rooted confidence in her innocence, in spite of her confession.

When the door was fast, Coppinger came over to Judith, and standing at a little distance from her, said—

" Judith—look at me."

She raised her eyes to him. He was pale and his face lined, but he had recovered greatly since that day when she had seen him suffering from the effects of the poison.

"Judith," said he, "I know all."

"What do you know?"

"You did not poison me."

"I mixed and prepared the bowl for you."

"Yes—but the poison had been put into the oatmeal before, not by you, not with your knowledge."

She was silent. She was no adept at lying. She could not invent another falsehood to convince him of her guilt.

"I know how it all came about," pursued Captain Coppinger. "The cook, Jane, has told me. Jamie came into the kitchen with a blue paper in his hand, asked for the oatmeal, and put in the contents of the paper so openly as not in the least to arouse suspicion. Not till I was taken ill and made inquiries did the woman connect his act with what followed. I have found the blue paper, and on it is written, in Mr. Menaida's handwriting, which I know: 'Arsenic. Poison: for Jamie, only to be used for the dressing of bird-skins, and a limited amount to be served to him at a time.' Now I am satisfied, because I know your character, and because I saw innocence in your manner when you came down to me on the second occasion —and dashed the bowl from my lips—I saw then that you were innocent."

Judith said nothing. Her eyes rested on the ground.

" I had angered that fool of a boy. I had beaten him. In a fit of sullen revenge, and without calculating either how best to do it, or what the consequences would be, he went to the place where he knew the arsenic was— Mr. Menaida had impressed on him the danger of playing with the poison—and he abstracted it. But he had not the wit or cunning generally present in idiots——"

" He is no idiot," said Judith.

" No, in fools," said Coppinger, "to put the poison into the oatmeal secretly when no one was in the kitchen. He asked the cook for the meal, and mingled the contents of the paper with it so openly as to disarm suspicion."

He paused for Judith to speak, but she did not. He went on—

"Then you, in utter guilelessness, prepared my breakfast for me, as instructed by Mrs. Trevisa. Next morning you did the same, but were either suspicious of evil through missing the paper from your cabinet, or drawer, or wherever you kept it, or else Jamie confessed to you what he had done. Thereupon you rushed to me, to save me from taking another portion. I do not know that I would have taken it—I had formed a half-suspicion from the burning sensation in my throat, and from what I saw in the spoon—but there was no doubt in my mind after the first discovery that you were guiltless. I sought the whole matter out, as far as I was able. Jamie is guilty—not you."

"And—," said Judith, drawing a long breath—"what about Jamie?"

"There are two alternatives," said Coppinger. "The boy is dangerous. Never again shall he come under my roof."

"No—," spoke Judith—"no, he must not go to the Glaze again. Let him remain here with me. I will take care of him that he does mischief to no one. He would never have hurt you had not you hurt him. Forgive him, because he was aggravated to it by the unjust and cruel treatment he received."

"The boy is a mischievous idiot," said Coppinger. "He must not be allowed to be at large."

"What, then, are your alternatives?"

"In the first place, I propose to send him back to that establishment whence he should never have been released—to Scantlebray's asylum."

"No—no—no!" gasped Judith. "You do not know what that place is. I do. I got into it. I saw how Jamie had been treated."

"He cannot be treated too severely. He is dangerous. You refuse this alternative?"

"Yes—indeed I do."

"Very well. Then I put the matter in the hands of justice, and he is proceeded against, and convicted of having attempted my life with poison. To gaol he will go."

It was as Judith had feared. There were but two destinations for Jamie—her dear, dear brother—the son of that blameless father—gaol or an asylum.

"Oh, no!—no—no! not that!" cried Judith.

"One or the other, and I give you six hours to choose," said Coppinger. Then he went to the door, opened it and stood looking seaward. Suddenly he started. " Hah! The *Black Prince!* " He turned in the door and said to Judith, "One hour after sunset come to Pentyre Glaze. Come alone, and tell me your decision. I will wait for that."

CHAPTER XLIX.

NOTHING LIKE GROG.

THE *Black Prince* had been observed by Oliver Menaida. He did not know for certain that the vessel he saw in the offing was the smuggler's ship, but he suspected it, as he knew that Coppinger was in daily expectation of her arrival. He brought his father to the cliffs, and the old man at once identified her.

Oliver considered what was to be done. A feint was to be made at a point lower down the coast, so as to attract the coastguard in that direction, whereas she was to run for Pentyre as soon as night fell, with all lights hidden, and to discharge her cargo in the little cove.

Oliver knew pretty well who were confederate with Coppinger or were in his employ. His father was able to furnish him with a good deal of information, not perhaps very well authenticated, all resting on gossip. He resolved to have a look at these men, and observe whether they were making preparations to assist Coppinger in clearing the *Black Prince* the moment she arrived off the cove. But he found that he had not far to look. They were drawn to the cliffs one after another to observe the distant vessel.

Oliver now made his way to the coastguard station, and to reach it went round by Wadebridge, and this he did because he wished to avoid being noticed going to the Preventive Station across the estuary at the Doom Bar above S. Enodoc. On reaching his destination, he was shown into an ante-room, where he had to wait some minutes, because the captain happened to be engaged. He had plenty to occupy his mind. There was that mysterious confession of Judith that she had tried to poison the man who persisted in considering himself as her husband, in spite of her resistance, and who was holding her in a condition of bondage in his house. Oliver did not for a moment believe that she had intentionally sought his life. He had seen enough of her to gauge her character, and he knew that she was incapable of committing a crime. That she might have given poison in ignorance and by accident was possible. How this had happened it was in vain for him to attempt to conjecture; he could, however, quite believe that an innocent and sensitive conscience like that of Judith might feel the pangs of self-reproach when hurt had come to Coppinger through her negligence.

Oliver could also believe that the smuggler captain attributed her act to an evil motive. He was not the man to believe in guilelessness; and when he found that he had been partly poisoned by the woman whom he daily tortured almost to madness, he would at once conclude that a premeditated attempt had been made on his life. What course would he pursue? Would he make this wretched business public, and bring a criminal action against the unfortunate and unhappy girl who was linked to him against her will?

Oliver saw that, if he could obtain Coppinger's arrest on some such a charge as smuggling, he might prevent this scandal, and save Judith from much humiliation and misery. He was, therefore, most desirous to effect the capture of Coppinger at once, and *flagrante delicto*.

As he waited in the ante-room a harsh voice within was audible which he recognized as that of Mr. Scantlebray. Presently the door was half opened, and he heard the coastguard captain say—

"I trust you rewarded the fellow for his information. You may apply to me——"

"Oh, royally, royally."

"And for furnishing you with the code of signals?"

"Imperially—imperially."

"That is well—never underpay in these matters."

"Do not fear! I emptied my pockets. And as to the information you have received through me—rely on it as you would on the Bank of England."

"You have been deceived and befooled," said Oliver, unable to resist the chance of delivering a slap at a man for whom he entertained a peculiar aversion, having heard much concerning him from his father.

"What do you mean?"

"That the shilling you gave the clerk for his information, and the half-crown for his signal-table, were worth what you got—the information was false, and was intended to mislead."

Scantlebray coloured purple.

"What do you know? You know nothing. You are in league with them."

"Take care what you say," said Oliver.

"I maintain," said Scantlebray, somewhat cowed by his demeanour, "that what I have said to the captain here is something of which you know nothing, and which is of importance for him to know."

"And I maintain that you have been hoodwinked," answered Oliver. "But it matters not. The event will prove which of us is on the right track."

"Yes," laughed Scantlebray, "so be it. And let me bet you, captain, and you, Mr. Oliver Menaida, that I am on the scent of something else. I believe I know where Coppinger keeps his stores, and—but you shall see, and Captain Cruel also—ha—ha!"

Rubbing his hands, he went out.

Then Oliver begged a word with the Preventive captain, and told him what he had overheard, and also that he knew where was the cave in which the smugglers had their boat and to which they ran the cargo first, before removing it to their inland stores.

"I'm not so certain the *Black Prince* dare venture nigh the coast to-night," said the captain, "because of the sea and the on-shore wind. But the glass is rising, and the wind may change. Then she'll risk it for certain. Now, look you here. I can't go with you myself to-night, because I must be here; and I can only let you have six men."

"That will suffice."

"Under Wyvill. I cannot, of course, put them under you, but Wyvill shall command. He bears a grudge against Coppinger, and will be rejoiced to have the chance of paying it out. But, mind you, it is possible that the *Black Prince* dare not run in, because of the weather, at Pentyre Cove; she may run somewhere else, either down the coast or higher up. Coppinger has other ovens than one. You know the term. His store places are ovens. We can't find them, but we know that there are several of them along the coast, just as there are a score of landing places. When one is watched, then another is used, and that is how we are thrown out. There are plenty of folk interested in defrauding the revenue in every parish between Hartland and Lands End, and let the *Black Prince* or any other smuggling vessel appear where she will, there she has ready helpers to shore her cargo and

convey it to the ovens. When we appear, it is sig-
-nalled at once to the vessel, and she runs away, up or
down the coast, and discharges somewhere else before
we can reach the point. Now, I do not say that what
you tell me is not true, and that it is not Coppinger's
intent to land the goods in the Pentyre Cove, but if we
are smelt, or if the wind or sea forbid a landing there,
away goes the *Black Prince* and runs her cargo somewhere else. That is why I cannot accompany you,
nor can I send you with more than half a dozen men.
I must be on the look out, and I must be prepared in
the event of her coming suddenly back and attempting
to land her goods at Porthleze, or Constantine, or
Harlyn. What you shall do is—remain here with me
till near dusk, and then you shall have a boat and
my men and get round Pentyre, and you shall take
possession of that cave. You shall take with you
provisions for twenty-four hours. If the *Black Prince*
intends to make that bay and discharge there, then
she will wait her opportunity. If she cannot to-night,
she will to-morrow night. Now, seize every man who
comes into that cave, and don't let him out. You
see ? "

" Perfectly."

" Very well. Wyvill shall be in command, and you shall be the guide, and I will speak to him to pay proper attention to what you recommend. You see ? "

" Exactly."

" Very well—now we shall have something to eat and to drink, which is better, and drink that is worth the drinking, which is best of all. Here is some cognac ; it was run goods that we captured and confiscated. Look at it. I wish there were artificial light and you would see, it is liquid amber—a liqueur. When you've tasted that, ' Ah-ha ! ' you will say, ' glad I lived to this moment.' There is all the difference, my boy, between your best cognac and common brandy. The one, the condensed sunshine in the queen of fruit sublimed to an essence ; the other, coarse, raw fire—all the difference that there is between a princess of blood-royal and a gipsy wench. Drink and do not fear. This is not the stuff to smoke the head and clog the stomach."

When Oliver Menaida finally started, he left the first officer of the coastguard, in spite of his assurances, somewhat smoky in brain, and not in the condition to form the clearest estimate of what should be done in a contingency. The boat was laden with provisions for twenty-four hours, and placed under the command of Wyvill.

The crew had not rowed far before one of them sang out, "Gearge!"

"Aye, aye, mate!" responded Wyvill.

"I say, Gearge. Be us a going round Pentyre?'

"I reckon we be."

"And wet to the marrow-bone we shall be."

"I reckon we shall."

Then a pause in the conversation. Presently from another—"George!"

"Aye, aye, Will!"

"I say, Gearge! Where be the spirits to? There's a keg o' water, but sure alive the spirits be forgotten."

"Bless my body!" exclaimed Wyvill, "I reckon you're right. Here's a go."

"It will never do for us to be twenty-four hours wi' salt water outside of us and fresh wi'in," said Will. "What's a hat wi'out a head in it, or boots wi'out feet in 'em, or a man wi'out spirits in his in'ar'd parts?"

"Dear alive! 'Tis a nuisance," said Wyvill. "Who's been the idiot to forget the spirits?"

" Gearge ! "

" Aye, aye, Samson ! "

" I say, Gearge ! Hadn't us better run over to the Rock, and get a little anker there ? "

" I reckon it wouldn't be amiss, mate," responded Wyvill.

To Oliver's astonishment and annoyance, the boat was turned to run across to a little tavern, at what was called " The Rock."

He remonstrated. This was injudicious and unnecessary.

" Onnecessary ! " said Wyvill. " Why, you don't suppose firearms will go off wi'out a charge ? It's the same wi' men. What's the good of a human being unless he be loaded—and what's his proper load but a drop o' spirits ? "

Then one of the rowers sang out—

> " Water drinkers are dull asses
>   When they're met together,
>   Milk is meet for infancy,
>   Ladies like to sip Bohea,
>   Not such stuff for you and me,
>   When we're met together."

Oliver was not surprised that so few captures were effected on the coast, when those set to watch it loved so dearly the very goods they were to watch against being importated untaxed.

On reaching the shore, the man Samson and another were left in charge of the boat, whilst Wyvill, Will, and the rest went up to the Rock Inn to have a glass for the good of the house, and to lade themselves with an anker of brandy, which during their wait in the cave was to be distributed among them. Oliver thought it well to go to the tavern as well. He was impatient, and thought they would dawdle there, and perhaps take more than the nip to which they professed themselves content to limit themselves. Pentyre Point had to be rounded in rough water, and they must be primed to enable them to round Pentyre. "You see," said Wyvill, who seemed to suppose that some sort of an explanation of his conduct was due. "When ropes be dry they be terrible slack. Wet 'em, and they are taut. It is the same wi' men's muscles. We've Pentyre Point to get round. Very strainin' to the arms, and I reckon it couldn't be done unless we wetted the muscles. That's reason. That's convincin'."

At the Rock Tavern the Preventive men found the clerk of S. Enodoc, with his hands in his pockets, on the settle, his legs stretched out before him considering one of his knees that was threadbare, and trying to make up his mind whether the trouser would hold out another day without a thread being run through the thin portion, and whether if a day, then perhaps two days, and if perchance for two days, then for three. But if for three, then why not for four? And if for four, then possibly for five. Anyhow, as far as he could judge, there was no immediate call for him to have the right knee of his trouser repaired that day.

The sexton-clerk looked up when the party entered, and greeted them each man by name, and a conversation ensued relative to the weather. Each described his own impressions as to what the weather had been, and his anticipations as to what it would be.

"And how's your missus?"

"Middlin', and yours?"

"Same, thanky'. A little troubled wi' the rheumatics."

"Tell her to take a lump o' sugar wi' five drops o' turpentine."

" I will, thanky',——" and so on for half an hour, at the end of which time the party thought it time to rise, wipe their mouths, shoulder the anker, and return to the boat. No sooner were they in it, and had thrust off from shore, and prepared to make a second start, than Oliver touched Wyvill and said, pointing to the land, " Look yonder."

" What ? "

" There is that clerk.   Running, actually running."

" I reckon he be."

" And in the direction of Pentyre."

" So he be, I reckon."

" And what do you think of that ? "

" Nothing," answered Wyvill, confusedly.   " Why should I ?   He can't say nothing about where we be going.   Not a word of that was said whilst us was there.   I don't put no store on his running."

" I do," said Oliver, unable to smother his annoy-ance.   " This folly will spoil our game."

Wyvill   muttered,   " I   reckon   I'm   head   of   the concarn, and not you."

Oliver deemed it advisable, as the words were said low, to pretend that he did not hear them.

The wind had somewhat abated, but the sea was running furiously round Pentyre. Happily the tide was going out, so that tide and wind were conflicting, and this enabled the rowers to get round Pentyre, between the Point and the Newland Isle, that broke the force of the seas. But when past the shelter of Newland, doubling a spur of Pentyre that ran to the north, the rowers had to use their utmost endeavours, and had not their muscles been moistened, they might possibly had declared it impossible to proceed. It was advisable to run into the cove just after dark, and before the turn of the tide, as, in the event of the *Black Prince* attempting to land her cargo there, it would be made with the flow of the tide, and in the darkness.

The cove was reached, and found to be deserted. Oliver showed the way, and the boat was driven up on the shingle, and conveyed into the Smugglers' Cave behind the rock curtain. No one was there. Evidently, from the preparations made, the smugglers were ready for the run of the cargo that night.

"Now," said Will, one of the Preventive men, "us hev 'a laboured uncommon. What say you,

Jamie was in good spirits, he chattered and laughed, and Judith made pretence that she listened; but her mind was absent, she had cares that had demands on every faculty of her mind. Moreover, now and then her thoughts drifted off to a picture that busy fancy painted and dangled before them—of Portugal, with its woods of oranges, golden among the burnished leaves, and its vines hung with purple grapes—with its glowing sun, its blue glittering sea—and, above all, she mused on the rest from fears, the cessation from troubles which would have ensued, had there been a chance for her to accept the offer made, and to have left the Cornish coast for ever.

Looking into the glowing ashes, listening to her thoughts as they spoke, and seeming to attend to the prattle of the boy, Judith was surprised by the entry of Mr. Scantlebray.

" There—disengaged, that is capital," said the agent. " The very thing I hoped. And now we can have a talk. You have never understood that I was your sincere friend. You have turned from me and looked elsewhere, and now you suffer for it. But I am like all the best metal—strong and bright to the last—and see—I have come to you now, to forewarn you, because I thought that if it came on you all at once, there would be trouble and bother."

"Thank you, Mr. Scantlebray. It is true that we are not busy just now, but it does not follow that we are disposed for a talk. It is growing dark, and we shall lock up the cottage and go to bed."

"Oh, I will not detain you long. Besides, I'll take the wish out of your heart for bed in one jiffy. Look here—read this. Do you know the handwriting?"

He held out a letter. Judith reluctantly took it. She had risen; she had not asked Scantlebray to take a seat.

"Yes," she said, "that is the writing of Captain Coppinger."

"A good bold hand," said the agent; "and see, here is his seal, with his motto *Thorough*. You know that?"

"Yes; it is his seal."

"Now read it."

Judith knelt at the hearth.

"Blow, blow the fire up, my beauty!" called Scantlebray to Jamie. "Don't you see that your sister wants light, and is running the risk of blinding her sweet pretty eyes."

Jamie puffed vigorously, and sent out sparks snapping and blinking, and brought the wood to a white glow, by which Judith was able to decipher the letter.

It was a formal order from Cruel Coppinger to Mr. Obadiah Scantlebray to remove James Trevisa that evening after dark from Othello Cottage to his idiot asylum, to remain there in custody till further notice. Judith remained kneeling with her eyes on the letter after she had read it. She was considering. It was clear to her that directly after leaving her Captain Coppinger had formed his own resolve, either impatient of waiting the six hours he had allowed her, or because he thought the alternative of the asylum the only one that could be accepted by her; and it was one that would content himself, as the only one that avoided exposure of a scandal. But there were other asylums than that of Scantlebray, and others were presumably better managed, and those in charge less severe in their dealings. She had considered this as she looked into the fire. But a new idea had also at the same time lightened in her mind, and she had a third alternative to propose.

She had been waiting for the moment when to go to the Glaze and see Coppinger, and just at the moment when she was about to send Jamie to bed and leave the house, Scantlebray came in.

" Now, then," said the agent, " what do you think of me? That I am a real friend? "

" I thank you for having told me this," answered Judith. " And now I will go to Pentyre. I beg that you will not allow my brother to be conveyed away during my absence. Wait till I return. Perhaps Captain Coppinger may not insist on the removal at once. If you are a real friend, as you profess, you will do this for me."

" I will do it willingly. That I am a real friend I have shown you by my conduct. I have come before-hand to break news to you which might have been too great and too overwhelming had it come on you suddenly. My brother and a man or two will be here in an hour. Go by all means to Captain Cruel, but—" Scantlebray winked an eye—" I don't myself think you will prevail with him."

"I will thank you to remain here for half an hour with Jamie," said Judith, coldly. "And to stay all proceedings till my return. If I succeed—well. If not, then only a few minutes have been lost. I have that to say to Captain Coppinger which may, and I trust will, lead him to withdraw that order."

"Rely on me. I am a rock on which you may build," said Scantlebray. "I will do my best to entertain your brother, though, alas! I have not the abilities of Obadiah, who is a genius, and can keep folks hour by hour going from one roar of laughter into another."

No sooner was Judith gone than Scantlebray put his tongue into one side of his cheek, clicked, pointed over his shoulder with his thumb, and seated himself opposite Jamie, on the stool beside the fire, which had been vacated by Judith. Jamie had understood nothing of the conversation that had taken place; his name had not been mentioned, and consequently his attention had not been drawn to it, away from some chestnuts he had found, or which had been given to him, that he was baking in the ashes on the hearth.

" Fond of hunting, eh ? " asked Scantlebray, stretching his legs, and rubbing his hands. " You are like me
—like to be in at the death. What do you suppose I
have in my pocket? Why, a fox with a fiery tail.
Shall we run him to earth? Shall we make an end
of him? Tally-ho! Tally-ho! here he is. Oh, sly
reynard, I have you by the ears." And forth from
the tail pocket of his coat Scantlebray produced a
bottle of brandy. " What say you, Corporal? shall
we drink his blood? Bring me a couple of glasses,
and I'll pour out his gore."

" I haven't any," said Jamie; " Ju and I have two
mugs, that is all."

" And they will do famously. Here goes—off with
the mask! " and with a blow he knocked away the
head and cork of the bottle. " No more running away
for you my beauty, except down our throats. Mugs!
That is famous. Come, shall we play at army and
navy, and the forfeit be a drink of reynard's blood ? "

Jamie pricked up his ears; he was always ready for
a game of play.

" Look here," said Scantlebray. " You are in the
military, I am in the nautical line. Each must address

the other by some title in accordance with the profession each professes, and the forfeit of failure is a pull at the bottle. What do you say? I will begin. Set the bottle there between us. Now then, Sergeant, they tell me your aunt has come in for a fortune. How much? What is the figure, eh?"

"I don't know," responded Jamie, and was at once caught up with " Forfeit! forfeit!"

"Oh, by Jimminy, there am I too in the same box. Take your swig, Commander, and pass to me."

"But what am I to call you?" asked the puzzle-headed boy.

"Mate, or captain, or boatswain, or admiral."

"I can't remember all that."

"That will do. Always say mate, whatever you ask or answer. Do you understand, General?"

"Yes."

"Forfeit! Forfeit!—you should have said, 'Yes, mate.'" Mr. Scantlebray put his hands to his sides and laughed.

"Oh, Jimminy! there am I again. The instructor as bad as the pupil. I'm a bad fellow as instructor, that I am, Field-Marshal. So—your Aunt Dionysia has come in for some thousands of pounds; how many do you think? Have you heard?"

"I think I've heard——"

"Mate! Mate!"

"I think I've heard, Mate."

"Now, how many do you remember to have heard named? Was it five thousand? That is what I heard named—eh, Captain?"

"Oh, more than that," said Jamie, in his small mind, catching at a chance of talking big, "a great lot more than that."

"What, ten thousand?"

"I dare say—yes, I think so."

"Forfeit! forfeit! pull again, Centurion."

"Yes, mate; I'm sure."

"Ten thousand—why at five per cent. that's a nice little sum for you and Ju to look forward to when the old hull springs a leak and goes to the bottom."

"Yes," answered Jamie, vaguely. He could not look beyond the day; moreover, he did not understand the figurative speech of his comrade.

"Forfeit again, general! but I'll forgive you this time, or you'll get so drunk you'll not be able to answer

me a question. Bless my legs and arms! on that
pretty little sum one could afford oneself a new tie
every Sunday. You will prove a beau and buck
indeed some day, Captain of thousands! And then
you won't live in this little hole. By the way, I hear
old Dunes Trevisa, I beg pardon, Field-Marshal Sir
James, I mean your much-respected aunt, Miss Trevisa,
has got a charming box down by S. Austell. You'll
ask me down for the shooting, won't you, Commander-
in-chief?"

"Yes, I will," answered Jamie.

"And you'll give me the best bedroom, and will
have choice dinners, and the best old tawny port,
eh?"

" Yes, to be sure," said the boy, flattered.

" Mate! mate! forfeit! and I suppose you'll keep a
hunter?"

" I shall have two—three," said Jamie.

" And if I were you I'd keep a pack of fox-hounds."

" I will."

" That's for the winter. And other hounds for the
summer."

" I am sure I will, and wear a red coat."

" Famous ; but—there I spare you this time—you forfeited again."

" No ; I won't be spared," protested the boy.

" As for a wretched little hole like this Othello Cottage——" said Scantlebray. "But, by the by, you have never shown me over the house. How many rooms are there in it, Generalissimo of His Majesty's Forces ? "

" There's my bedroom, there," said Jamie.

" Yes ; and that door leads to your sister's ? "

" Yes. And there's the kitchen."

" And upstairs ? "

" There's no upstairs."

" Now, you are very clever, clever. By Ginger, you must be to be Commander-in-chief, but upon my word, I can't believe that. No upstairs ? There must be upstairs."

" No, there's not."

" But, by Jimminy ! with such a roof as this house has got, and a little round window in the gable, there must be an upstairs."

" No, there's not."

" How do you make that out ? "

" Because there are no stairs at all." Then Jamie jumped up, but rolled on one side; the brandy he had drunk had made him unsteady. " I'll show you, mate—mate—yes, mate. There, three times now will do for times I haven't said it. There—in my room. The floor is rolling; it won't stay steady. There are cramps in the wall—no stairs, and so you get up to where it all is."

" All what is ? "

" Forfeit ! forfeit ! " shouted Jamie. " Say general or something military. I don't know; Ju won't let me go up there; but there's tobacco, for one thing."

" Where's a candle, Corporal ? "

" There is none. We have no light but the fire. Then Jamie dropped back on his stool, unable to keep his legs.

" I am more provident than you. I have a lantern outside, unlighted, as I thought I might need it on my return. The nights close in very fast and very dark now, eh, Commander ? "

Mr. Scantlebray went outside the cottage, looked about him, specially directing his eyes towards the Glaze. Then he chuckled and said—

"Sent Miss Judith on a wild goose chase, have I? Ah! ha! Captain Coppinger! I'll have a little entertainment for you to-night. The Preventives will snatch your goods at Porth-leze or Constantine, and here—behind your back—I'll attend to your store of tobacco and whatever else I may find."

Then he returned, and going to the fire, extracted the candle from the lantern, and lighted it at a burning log.

"Halloa, Captain of thousands! Going to sleep? There's the bottle. You must make up forfeits. You've been dishonest, I fear, and not paid half. That door did you say?"

But Jamie was past understanding a question, and Mr. Scantlebray could find out for himself now what he wanted to know. That this house had been used by Coppinger as a store for some of the smuggled cargoes he had long suspected, but he had never been able to obtain any evidence which would justify the coastguard in applying to the justices for a search warrant. Now he would be able to look about it at his leisure whilst Judith was absent. He did not suppose Coppinger was at the Glaze. He assumed that an attempt would be made, as the clerk of S.

Enodoc had informed him, to land the cargo of the *Black Prince* to the west of the estuary of the Camel, and he supposed that Coppinger would be there to superintend. He had used the letter sent to his brother to induce the girl to go to Pentyre, and so leave the cottage clear for him to search it.

Now, holding the candle, he entered the bedroom of Jamie, and soon perceived the cramps the boy had spoken of, that served in place of stairs. Above was a door into the attic, whitewashed over, like the walls. Mr. Scantlebray climbed, thrust open the door, and crept into the garret.

" Ha, ha ! " said the valuer. " So, so, Captain ! I have come on one of your lairs at last. And I reckon I will make it warm for you. But, by Ginger, it is a pity I can't remove some of what is here."

He prowled about in the roomy loft, searching every corner. There were a few small kegs of spirit, but the stores were mostly of tobacco.

In about ten minutes Mr. Scantlebray reappeared in the room where was Jamie. He was without his candle. The poor boy, overcome by what he had drunk, had fallen on the floor, and was in a tipsy sleep.

Scantlebray went to him.

"Come along with me," he said. "Come, there is no time to be lost. Come, you fool!"

He shook him, but Jamie would not be roused; he kicked and struck out with his fists.

"You won't come? I'll make you."

Then Scantlebray caught the boy by the shoulders to drag him to the door. The child began to struggle and resist.

"Oh, I'm not concerned for you, fool," said Scantlebray. "If you like to stay and take your chance —— My brother will be here to carry you off presently. Will you come?"

Scantlebray caught the boy by the feet and tried to drag him, but Jamie clung to the table legs.

Scantlebray uttered an oath. "Stay, you fool, and be smothered! The world will get on very well without you." And he strode forth from the cottage.

CHAPTER LI.

SURRENDER.

SCANTLEBRAY was mistaken. Coppinger had not crossed the estuary of the Camel. He was at Pentyre Glaze awaiting the time when the tide suited for landing the cargo of the *Black Prince*. In the kitchen were a number of men having their supper, and drinking, waiting also for the proper moment when to issue forth.

At the turn of the tide the *Black Prince* would approach in the gathering darkness, and would come as near in as she dare venture. The wind had fallen, but the sea was running, and with the tide setting in, she would approach the cove.

Judith hastened towards the Glaze. Darkness had set in, but in the north were auroral lights, first a great white halo, then rays that shot up to the zenith, and then a mackerel sky of rosy light. The growl and mutter of the sea filled the air with threat, like an angry multitude surging on with blood and destruction in their hearts.

The flicker overhead gave Judith light for her course, the snow had melted except in ditches and under hedges, and there it glared red or white in response to the changing luminous tinges of the heavens. When she reached the house she at once entered the hall; there Coppinger was awaiting her. He knew she would come to him when her mind was made up on the alternatives he had offered her, and he believed he knew pretty surely which she would choose. It was because he expected her that he had not suffered the men, collected for the work of this night, to invade the hall.

" You are here," he said. He was seated by the fire. He looked up, but did not rise. " Almost too late."

" Almost, maybe — but not altogether," answered Judith. " And yet it seems unnecessary, as you have already acted without awaiting my decision."

" What makes you say that ? "

" I have been shown your letter."

"Oh! Obadiah Scantlebray is premature."

"He is not at Othello Cottage yet. His brother came beforehand to prepare me."

"How considerate of your feelings!" sneered Captain Cruel; "I would not have expected that of Scantlebray."

"You have not awaited my decision," said Judith.

"That is true," answered Coppinger, carelessly. "I knew you would shrink from the exposure, the disgrace, of publication of what has occurred here—I knew you so well, that I could reckon beforehand on what you would elect."

"But, why to Scantlebray? Are there not other asylums?"

"Yes; so long as that boy is placed where he can do no mischief, I care not."

"Then, if that be so, I have another proposal to make."

"What is that?" Coppinger stood up.

"If you have any regard for my feelings, any care for my happiness, you will grant my request."

"Let me hear it."

"Mr. Menaida is going to Portugal."

"What!"—in a tone of concentrated rage—"Oliver?"

"Oliver and his father. But the proposal concerns the father."

"Go on." Coppinger strode once across the room, then back again. "Go on," he said, savagely.

"Old Mr. Menaida offers to take Jamie with him. He intends to settle at Oporto, near his son, who has been appointed to a good situation there. He will gladly undertake the charge of Jamie. Let Jamie go with them. There he can do no harm."

"What, go—without you? Did they not want you to go also?"

Judith hesitated and flushed. There was a single tallow candle on the table. Coppinger took it up, snuffed it, and held the flame to her face, to study its expression.

"I thought so," he said, and put down the light again.

"Jamie is useful to Mr. Menaida," pleaded Judith, in some confusion, and with a voice of tremulous apology. "He stuffs birds so beautifully, and Uncle Zachie—I mean Mr. Menaida—has set his heart on making a collection of the Spanish and Portuguese birds."

"Oh, yes; he understands the properties of arsenic," said Coppinger, with a scoff.

Judith's eyes fell. Captain Cruel's tone was not reassuring.

"You say that you care not where Jamie be, so long as he is where he cannot hurt you," said Judith.

"I did not say that," answered Coppinger. "I said that he must be placed where he can injure no one."

"He can injure no one if he is with Mr. Menaida, who will well watch him, and keep him employed."

Coppinger laughed bitterly. "And you? Will you be satisfied to have the idolized brother with the deep seas rolling between you?"

"I must endure it; it is the least of evils."

"But you would be pining to have wings and fly over the sea to him."

"If I have not wings, I cannot go."

"Now hearken," said Coppinger. He clenched his fist and laid it on the table. "I know very well what this means. Oliver Menaida is at the bottom of this. It is not the fool Jamie who is wanted in Portugal, but the clever Judith. They have offered to take the boy, that through him they may attract you, unless"—his voice thrilled—"they have already dared to propose that you should go with them."

Judith was silent. Coppinger clenched his second hand and laid that also on the table.

"I swear to Heaven," said he, "that if I and that Oliver Menaida meet again, it is for the last time for one or other of us. We have met twice already. It is an understood thing between us, when we meet again, one wets his boots in the other's blood. Do you hear? The world will not hold us two any longer. Portugal may be far off, but it is too near Cornwall for me."

Judith made no answer. She looked fixedly into the gloomy eyes of Coppinger, and said—

"You have strange thoughts. Suppose, if you will, that the invitation included me, I could not have accepted it."

"Why not? You refuse to regard yourself as married—and, if unmarried, you are free—and, if free, ready to elope with——"

He would not utter the name, in his quivering fury.

"I pray you," said Judith, offended, "do not insult me."

"I—insult you? It is a daily insult to me to be treated as I have been. It is driving me mad."

"But, do you not see," urged Judith; "you have offered me two alternatives, and I ask for a third; yours are gaol or an asylum; mine is exile. Both yours are to me intolerable. Conceive of my state were Jamie either in gaol or with Mr. Scantlebray! In gaol—and I should be thinking of him all day and all night, in his prison garb, tramping the tread-mill, beaten, driven on, associated with the vilest of men, an indelible stain put not on him only, but on the name of our dear, dear father. Do you think I could bear that? Or take the other alternative. I know the Scantlebrays. I would have the thoughts of Jamie distressed, frightened, solitary, ill-treated, ever before me. I had it for a few hours once, and it drove me frantic. It would make me mad in a week. I know that I could not endure it. Either alternative would madden or kill me. And I offer another—if he were in exile, I could at least think of him as happy, among the orange groves, in the vineyards, among kind friends, happy, innocent—at worst, forgetting me. *That* I could bear. But the other—no, not for a week—they would be torture insufferable."

She spoke full of feverish vehemence, with her hands outspread before her.

"And this smiling vision of Jamie happy in Portugal would draw your heart from me."

"You never had my heart," said Judith.

Coppinger clenched his teeth. "I will hear no more of this," said he.

Then Judith threw herself on her knees, and caught him and held him, lifting her entreating face towards his.

"I have undergone it—for some hours. I know it will madden or kill me. I cannot—I cannot—I cannot." She could scarce breathe; she spoke in gasps.

"You cannot what?" he asked, sullenly.

"I cannot live on the terms you offer. You take from me even the very wish to live. Take away the arsenic from me, lest in madness I give it to myself. Take me far inland from these cliffs, lest in my madness I throw myself over—I could not bear it. Will nothing move you?"

"Nothing." He stood before her, his feet apart, his arms folded, his chin on his breast, looking into her uplifted, imploring face. "Yes—one thing. One thing only." He paused, raking her face with his eyes.

" Yes—one thing. Be mine wholly—unconditionally. Then I will consent. Be mine ; add your name where it is wanting. Resume your ring—and Jamie shall go with the Menaidas. Now, choose."

He drew back. Judith remained kneeling, upright, on the floor with arms extended ; she had heard, and at first hardly comprehended him. Then she staggered to her feet.

" Well," said Coppinger, " what answer do you make ? "

Still she could not speak. She went to the table with uncertain steps. There was a wooden form by it. She seated herself on this, placed her arms on the table-board, joining her hands, and laid her head, face downwards, between them on the table.

Coppinger remained where he was, watching and waiting. He knew what her action implied—that she was to be left alone with her thoughts, to form her resolve undisturbed.

He remained, accordingly, motionless, but with his eyes fixed on the golden hair, that flickered in the dim light of the one candle. The wick had a great fungus in it—so large and glowing that in another moment it would fall, and fall on Judith's hand. Coppinger saw this, and he thrust forth his arm to snuff the candle with his fingers, but his hand shook, and the light was extinguished. It mattered not. There were glowing coals on the hearth, and through the window flared and throbbed the auroral lights.

A step sounded outside. Then a hand was on the door. Coppinger at once strode across the hall, and arrested the intruder from entering.

"Who is that?"

"Hender Pendarvis"—the clerk of S. Enodoc. "I have som'ut partickler I must say."

Coppinger looked at Judith; she lay motionless, her head between her arms, on the board. He partly opened the door, and stepped forth into the porch.

When he had heard what the clerk of S. Enodoc had to say, he answered with an order—

"Round to the kitchen, bid the men arm, and go by the beach."

He returned into the hall, went to the fireplace, and took down a pair of pistols, tried them, that they were charged, and thrust them into his belt. Next he went up to Judith, and laid his hand on her shoulder.

" Time presses," he said ; " I have to be off.   Your answer."

She looked up.   The board was studded with drops of water.   She had not wept ; these stains were not her tears, they were the sweat of anguish off her brow that had run over the board.

" Well, Judith, your answer."

" I accept."

" Unreservedly ? "

" Unreservedly."

" Stay," said he.   He spoke low, in distinctly articulated sentences.   " Let there be no holding back between us—you shall know all.   You have wondered concerning the death of Wyvill—I know you have asked questions about it.   I killed him."

He paused.

" You heard of the wreckers on that vessel cast on Doom Bar.   I was their leader."

Again he paused.

" You thought I had sent Jamie out with a light to mislead the vessel.   You thought right.   I did have her drawn to her destruction—and by your brother."

He paused again.   He saw Judith's hand twitch that was the only sign of emotion in her.

"And Lady Knighton's jewels. I took them off her —it was I who tore her ear."

Again a stillness. The sky outside shone in at the window, a lurid red. From the kitchen could be heard the voice of a man singing.

"Now you know all," said Coppinger. "I would not have you take me finally, fully, unreservedly without knowing the truth. Give me your resolve."

She slightly lifted her hands; she looked steadily into his face with a stony expression in hers.

"What is it?"

"I cannot help myself—unreservedly yours."

Then he caught her to him, pressed her to his heart, and kissed her wet face — wet as though she had plunged it into the sea.

"To-morrow," said he—"to-morrow shall be our true wedding."

And he dashed out of the house.

CHAPTER LII.

TO JUDITH.

IN the smugglers' cave were Oliver Menaida and the party of Preventive men, not under his charge, but under that of Wyvill. This man, though zealous in the execution of his duty, and not averse, should the opportunity offer, of paying off a debt in full with a bullet, instead of committing his adversary to the more lenient hands of the law, shared in that failing, if it were a failing, of being unable to do anything without being primed with spirits, a failing that was common at that period to coastguards and smugglers alike. The latter had to be primed in order to run a cargo, and the former must be in like condition to catch them at it. It was thought, not unjustly, that the magistrates before whom, if caught, the smugglers were brought, needed

priming in order to ripen their intellects for pro-
nouncing judgment. But it was not often that a
capture was effected. When it was, priming was
allowed for the due solemnization of the fact by the
captors ; failure always entitled them to priming in
order to sustain their disappointment with fortitude.
Wyvill had lost a brother in the cause, and his feelings
often overcame him when he considered his loss, and
their poignancy had to be slaked with the usual priming.
It served, as its advocates alleged, as a great stimulant
to courage ; but it served also, as its deprecators asserted, as a solvent to discipline.

Now that the party were in possession of the den of
their adversaries, such a success needed, in their eyes,
commemoration. They were likely, speedily, to have a
tussle with the smugglers, and to prepare themselves
for that required the priming of their nerves and sinews.
They had had a sharp struggle with the sea in rounding
Pentyre Point, and their unstrung muscles and joints
demanded screwing up again by the same means.

The *Black Prince* had been discerned through the
falling darkness drawing shorewards with the rising
tide ; but it was certain that for another hour or two

the men would have to wait before she dropped anchor, and before those ashore came down to the unloading.

A lantern was lighted, and the cave was explored. Certainly Coppinger's men from the land would arrive before the boats from the *Black Prince,* and it was determined to at once arrest them, and then await the contingent in the boats, and fall on them as they landed. The party was small, it consisted of but seven men, and it was advisable to deal with the smugglers piecemeal.

The men, having leisure, brought out their food, and tapped the keg they had procured at the Rock. It was satisfactory to them that the *Black Prince* was apparently bent on discharging her cargo that night and in that place, thus, they would not have to wait in the cave twenty-four hours, and not, after all, be disappointed.

"All your pistols charged?" asked Wyvill.

"Aye, aye, sir."

"Then take your suppers whilst you may. We shall have hot work presently. Should a step be heard below, throw a bit o' sailcloth over the lantern, Samson."

Oliver was neither hungry nor thirsty. He had both eaten and drunk sufficient when at the station. He

therefore left the men to make their collation, prime
their spirits, pluck up their courage, screw up their
nerves, polish their wits, all with the same instrument,
and descended the slope of shingle, stooped under the
brow of rock that divided the lower from the upper cave,
and made his way to the entrance, and thence out over
the sands of the cove. He knew that the shore could
be reached only by the donkey path, or by the dangerous
track down the chimney—a track he had not discovered
till he had made a third exploration of the cave. Down
this tortuous and perilous descent he was convinced the
smugglers would not come. It was, he saw, but rarely
used, and designed as a way of escape only on an
emergency. A too frequent employment of this path
would have led to a treading of the turf on the cliff
above, and to a marking of the line of descent, that
would have attracted the attention of the curious, and
revealed to the explorer the place of retreat.

Oliver, therefore, went forward towards the point
where the donkey path reached the sands, deeming it
advisable that a watch should be kept on this point, so
that his party might be forewarned in time of the approach of the smugglers.

There was much light in the sky, a phantastic, mysterious glow, as though some great conflagration were taking place, and the clouds overhead reflected its flicker. There passed throbs of shadow from side to side, and, as Oliver looked, he could almost believe that the light he saw proceeded from a great bonfire, such as was kindled on the Cornish moors on Midsummer's Eve, and that the shadows were produced by men and women dancing round the flames and momentarily intercepting the light.

Then ensued a change—the rose hue vanished suddenly, and in its place shot up three broad ribands of silver light, and so bright and clear was the light that the edge of the cliff against it was cut as sharp as a black silhouette on white paper, and he could see every bush of gorse there, and a sheep—a solitary sheep.

Suddenly he was startled by seeing a man before him, coming over the sand.

" Who goes there ? "

" What, Oliver ! I have found you ! " The answer was in his father's voice. " Oh, well, I got fidgeted, and I thought I would come and see if you had arrived."

"For Heaven's sake! you have told no one of our plans?"

"I—bless you, boy!—not I. You know you told me yourself, before going to the station, what you intended, and I was troubled and anxious, and I came to see how things were turning out. The *Black Prince* is coming in; she will anchor shortly. She can't come beyond the point yonder. I was sure you would be here. How many have you brought with you?"

"But six."

"Too few. However, now I am with you, that makes eight."

"I wish you had not come, father."

"My boy, I did not come only on your account. I have my poor little Ju so near my heart, that I long to put out if only a finger to liberate her from that ruffian, whom, by the way, I have challenged."

"Yes; but I have stepped in as your substitute. I shall, I trust, try conclusions with Coppinger to-night. Come with me to the cave I told you of. We will send a man to keep guard at the foot of the donkey path."

Oliver led the way; the sands reflected the illumination of the sky, and the foam that swept up the beach had a rosy tinge. The waves hissed as they rushed up the shore, as though impatient at men speaking and not listening to the voice of the ocean, that should subdue all human tongues, and command mute attention. And yet that roar is inarticulate, it is like the foaming fury of the dumb, that strives with noise and gesticulation to explain the thoughts that are working within.

In the cave it was dark, and Oliver lighted a piece of touchwood as a means of observing the shelving ground and taking his direction till he passed under the brow of rock and entered the upper cavern.

After a short scramble, the dim, yellow glow of light from this inner recess was visible, when Oliver extinguished his touchwood and pushed on, guided by this light.

On entering the upper cave he was surprised to find the guards lying about asleep and snoring. He went at once to Wyvill, seized him by the arm and shook him, but none of his efforts could rouse him. He lay as a log, or as one stunned.

"Father, help me with the others," said Oliver, in great concern.

Mr. Menaida went from one to the other, spoke to each, shook him, held the lantern to his eyes, he raised their heads, when he let go his hold they fell back.

" What is the meaning of this ? " asked Oliver.

" Humph ! " said old Menaida, " I'll tell you what this means : there is a rogue among them, and their drink has been drugged with deadly-nightshade. You might be sure of this—that among six coastguards one would be in the pay of Coppinger. Which is it ? Whoever it is he is pretending to be as dead drunk and stupefied as the others, and which is the man, Noll ? "

" I cannot tell. This keg of brandy was got at the Rock Inn."

" It was got there, and there drugged, but by one of this company. Who is it ? "

" Yes," said Oliver, waxing wrathful, " and what is more, notice was sent to Coppinger to be on his guard. I saw the sexton going in the direction of Pentyre."

" That man is a rascal ! "

" And now we shall not encounter Coppinger. He will be warned, and not come."

" Trust him to come. He has heard of this. He will come, and murder them all, as he did Wyvill."

Oliver felt as though a frost had fallen on him.

"Hah!" said old Menaida. "Never trust any one in this neighbourhood; you cannot tell who is not in the pay or under the control of Coppinger, from the magistrate on the bench to the huckster who goes round the country. Among these six men one is a spy and a traitor. Which it is we cannot tell. There is nothing else to be done but to bind them all, hand and foot. There is plenty of cord here."

"Plenty. But surely not Wyvill."

"Wyvill and all. How can you say that he is not the man who has done it? Many a fellow has carried his brother in his pocket. What if he has been bought?"

Old Menaida was right. He had not lived so many years in the midst of smugglers without having learned something of their ways. His advice must be taken, for the danger was imminent. If, as he supposed, full information had been sent to Captain Cruel, then he and his men would be upon them shortly.

Oliver hastily brought together all the cord of a suitable thickness he could find, and the old father raised and held each Preventive man, whilst Oliver firmly bound him hand and foot. As he did not know which was shamming sleep he must bind all. Of the six, five were wholly unconscious what was being done to them, and the sixth thought it advisable to pretend to be as the rest, for he was quite aware that neither Oliver nor his father would scruple to silence him effectually did he show signs of animation.

When all were made fast, old Menaida said—

"Now, Noll, my boy, are you armed?"

"No, father. When I went from home I expected to return. I did not know I should want weapons. But these fellows have their pistols and cutlasses."

"Try the pistols. There, take that of the man Wyvill. Are you sure they are loaded?"

"I know they are."

"Well, try."

Oliver took Wyvill's pistol, and put in the ramrod.

"Oh yes, it is loaded."

"Make sure. Draw the loading. You don't know what it is to have to do with Coppinger."

Oliver drew the charge, and then, as is usual, when the powder has been removed, blew down the barrel. Then he observed that there was a choke somewhere.

He took the pistol to the lantern, opened the side of the lantern, and examined it.   The touch-hole was plugged with wax.

"Humph!" said Mr. Menaida, "the man who drugged the liquor waxed the touch-holes of the pistols.   Try the rest."

Oliver did not now trouble himself to draw the charges, he cocked each man's pistol, and drew the trigger.   Not one would discharge.   All had been treated in like manner.

Oliver thought for a moment what was to be done. He dared not leave the sleeping men unprotected, and he and his father alone were insufficient to defend them.

"Father," said he, "there is but one thing that can be done now : you must go at once, fly to the nearest farm-houses and collect men, and, if possible, hold the donkey path before Coppinger and his men arrive.   If you are too late, pursue them.   I will choke the narrow entrance, and will light a fire.   Perhaps they may be afraid when they see a blaze here, and may hold off. Anyhow, I can defend this place for a while.   But I don't expect that they will attack it."

Mr. Menaida at once saw that his son's judgment.

was right, and he hurried out of the cave, Oliver holding the light to assist him to descend, and then he made his way over the sands to the path, and up that to the downs.

No sooner was he gone than Oliver collected what wood and straw were there, sailcloth, oilcloth, everything that was combustible, and piled them up into a heap, then applied the candle to them, and produced a flame. The wood was damp, and did not burn freely, but he was able to awake a good fire, that filled the cavern with light. He trusted that when the smugglers saw that their den was in the possession of the enemy they would not risk the attempt to enter and recover it. They might not, they probably did not, know to what condition the holders of the cave were reduced.

The light of the fire roused countless bats that had made the roof of the cave their resting-place, and they flew wildly to and fro with whirr of wings and shrill screams.

Oliver set to work with all haste to heap stones so as to choke the entrance from the lower cave, by which he anticipated that the smugglers would enter, should they resolve on so desperate a course. But, owing to the rapid inclination, the pebbles yielded, and what he piled up rolled down. He then, with great effort, got the boat thrust down to the opening, and by main force drew it partly across. It was not possible for him completely to block the entrance, but by planting the boat athwart it, he could prevent several men from entering at once, and whoever did enter must scramble over the bulwarks of the boat.

All this took some time, and he was thus engaged, when his attention was suddenly arrested by the click of a pistol brought to the cock. He looked hastily about him, and saw Coppinger, who, unobserved, had descended by the chimney, and now by the light of the fire was taking deliberate aim at him. Oliver drew back behind a rock.

"You coward!" shouted Captain Cruel. "Come out and be shot."

"I am no coward," answered Oliver. "Let us meet with equal arms; I have a cutlass." He had taken one from the side of one of a sleep-drunk coast-guard.

"I prefer to shoot you down as a dog," said Coppinger.

Then, holding his pistol levelled in the direction of Oliver, he approached the sleeping men. Oliver saw at once his object—he would liberate the confederate. He stepped out from behind the rock, and immediately the pistol was discharged. A bat fell at the feet of Oliver. Had not that bat at the moment whizzed past his head and received the ball in its soft and yielding body, the young man would have fallen shot through the head.

Coppinger uttered a curse and put his hand to his belt and drew forth the second pistol. But Oliver sprang forward, and with a sweep of his cutlass caught him on the wrist with the blade as he was about to touch the trigger. The pistol fell from his hand, and a rush of blood overflowed the back of the hand.

Coppinger remained for one minute motionless. So did Oliver, who did not again raise his cutlass.

But at that moment a harsh voice was heard crying, "There he is, my men, at him; beat his brains out. A guinea for the first man who knocks him over," and from the further side of the boat illumined by the glare from the fire, were seen the faces of Mr. Scantlebray, his brother, and several men, who began to scramble over the obstruction.

Then, and then only in his life, did Coppinger's heart fail him. His right hand was powerless, the sharp blade had severed the tendons, and blood was flowing from his wrist in streams. One pistol was discharged, the other had fallen. In a minute he would be in the hands of his deadly enemies.

He turned and fled. The light from the fire, the illumined smoke, rose through the chimney, and by that he could run up the familiar track, reach the platform in the face of the cliff, thence make his way by the path up which he had formerly borne Judith. He did not hesitate, he fled, and Oliver, also without hesitation, pursued him. As he went up the narrow track, his feet trod in and were stained with the blood that had fallen from Coppinger's wounded arm, but he did not notice it—he was unaware of it till the morrow.

Coppinger reached the summit of the cliffs. His feet were on the down. He ran at once in the direction of Othello Cottage. His only chance of safety lay there. There he could hide in the attic, and Judith would never betray him. In his desperate condition, wounded, his blood flowing from him in streams, hunted by his foes, that one thought was in him— Judith—he must go to Judith.   She would never betray him, she would be hacked to death rather than give him up.   To Judith as his last refuge !

CHAPTER LIII.

IN THE SMOKE.

JUDITH left Pentyre Glaze when she had somewhat recovered herself after the interview with Coppinger and her surrender. She had fought a brave battle, but had been defeated and must lay down her arms. Resistance was no longer possible, if Jamie was to be saved from a miserable fate. Now, by the sacrifice of herself, she had assured to him a future of calm and innocent happiness. She knew that with Uncle Zachie and Oliver he would be cared for, kindly treated, and employed. Uncle Zachie himself was not to be trusted; whatever he might promise, his good nature was greater than his judgment. But she had confidence in Oliver, who would prove a check on the over-indulgence which his father would allow. But

Jamie would forget her. His light and unretentive mind was not one to harbour deep feeling. He would forget her when on board ship, in his pleasure at running about the vessel, chattering with the sailors ; and would only think of her if he wanted aught, or was ill. Rapidly the recollection of her, love for her, would die out of his mind and heart, and as it died out of his, her thought and love for him would deepen and become more fixed, for she would have no one, nothing in the world, to think of and love save her twin brother.

She walked on, in the dark winter night, lighted only by the auroral glow overhead, and was conscious of a smell of tobacco-smoke, that so persistently seemed to follow her, that she was forced to notice it. She became uneasy, thinking that some one was walking behind the hedge with a pipe, watching her, perhaps waiting to spring out upon her, when distant from the house where her cries for help might be heard.

She stood still. The smell was strong. She climbed the hedge on one side and looked over ; as far as she could discern in the red glimmer from the flushed sky, there was no one there. She listened, she could hear no step. She walked hastily on to a gate in the hedge on the opposite side, and went through that. The smell of burning tobacco was as strong there. Judith turned in the lane and walked back in the direction of the house. The smell pursued her. It was strange. Could she carry the odour in her clothes? She turned again, and resumed her walk towards Othello Cottage. Now she was distinctly aware that the scent came to her on the wind. Her perplexity on this subject served as a diversion of her mind from her own troubles.

She emerged upon the downs, and made her way across them towards the cottage, that lay in a dip, not to be observed except by one close to it. The wind when it brushed up from the sea was odourless.

Presently she came in sight of Othello Cottage, and in spite of the darkness could see that a strange, dense white fog surrounded it, especially the roof, which seemed to be wearing a white wig. In a moment she understood what this signified. Othello Cottage was on fire, and the stores of tobacco in the attic were burning. Judith ran. Her own troubles were forgotten in her alarm for Jamie. No fire as yet had broken through the roof.

She reached the door, which was open. Mr. Scantle-

bray in leaving had not shut the door, so as to allow
the boy to crawl out, should he recover sufficient
intelligence to see that he was in danger.

It is probable that Scantlebray senior would have
made further efforts to save Jamie, but that he believed
he would meet with his brother and two or three men
he was bringing with him near the house, and then it
would be easy unitedly to drag the boy forth. He did,
indeed, meet with Obadiah, but also, at the same time,
with Uncle Zachie Menaida, and a small party of
farm labourers, and when he heard that Mr. Menaida
desired help to secure Coppinger and the smugglers,
he thought no more of the boy, and joined heartily in
the attempt to rescue the Preventive men, and take
Coppinger.

Through the open door dashed Judith, crying out to
Jamie, whom she could not see. There was a dense
white cloud in the room, let down from above and
curling out at the top of the door, whence it issued as
steam from a boiler. It was impossible to breathe in
this fog of tobacco smoke, and Judith knew that if she
allowed it to surround her, she would be stupefied.
She therefore stooped and entered, calling Jamie.

Although the thick matrass of white smoke had not as yet descended to the floor, and that it left comparatively clear air beneath it—the indraught from the door, yet the odour of the burning tobacco impregnated the atmosphere. Here and there curls of smoke descended, dropped capriciously from the bed of vapour above, and wantonly played about.

Judith saw her brother lying at full length near the fire. Scantlebray had drawn him partly to the door, but he had rolled back to his former position near the hearth, perhaps from feeling the cold wind that blew in on him.

There was no time to be lost. Judith knew that flame must burst forth directly—directly the burning tobacco had charred through the rafters and flooring of the attic, and allowed the fresh air from below to rush in, and, acting as a bellows, blow the whole mass of glowing tobacco into flame. It was obvious that the fire had originated above, in the attic. There was nothing burning in the room, and the smoke drove downward in strips, through the joints of the boards overhead.

" Jamie ! come, come with me ! "   She shook the

boy, she knelt by him and raised him on her knee. He was stupefied with cognac, and with the fumes of the burning tobacco he had inhaled.

She must drag him forth. He was no longer half conscious as he had been when Mr. Scantlebray made the same attempt; the power to resist was now gone from him.

Judith was delicately made, and was not strong, but she put her arms under the shoulders of Jamie, and, herself on her knees, dragged him along the floor. He was as heavy as a corpse. She drew him a little way, and desisted, overcome, panting, giddy, faint. But time must not be lost. Every moment was precious. Judith knew that overhead, in the loft, was something that would not smoulder and glow, but burst into furious flame—spirits. Not, indeed, many kegs, but there were some. When this became ignited, their escape would be impossible. She drew Jamie further up, she was behind him. She thrust him forward as she moved on, upon her knees, driving him a step further at every advance. It was slow and laborious work. She could not maintain this effort for long, and fell forwards on her hands, and he fell also, at the same time, on the floor.

Then she heard a sound, a roar, an angry growl. The shock of the fall, and striking his head against the slate pavement, roused Jamie momentarily, and he also heard the noise.

" Ju! the roar of the sea!"

"A sea of fire, Jamie! Oh, do push to the door."

He raised himself on his hands, looked vacantly round, and fell again into stupid unconsciousness. Now, still on her knees, but with a brain becoming bewildered with the fumes, she crept to his head, placed herself between him and the door, and, holding his shoulders, dragged him towards her, she moving backwards.

Even thus she could make but little way with him; his boot-tops caught in the edge of a slate slab, ill-fitted in the floor, and held him, so that she could not pull him to her with the addition of the resistance thus caused. Then an idea struck her. Staggering to her feet, holding her breath, she plunged in the direction of the window, beat it open, and panted in the inrush of pure air. With this new current wafted in behind her she returned amidst the smoke, and for a moment it dissipated the density of the cloud about her. The

window had faced the wind, and the rush of air through
it was more strong than that which entered by the
door. And yet this expedient did not answer as she
had expected, for the column of strong cold air pouring
in from a higher level threw the cloud into confusion,
stirred it up, as it were, and lessened the space of un-
invaded atmosphere below the descending bed of
vapour.

Again she went to Jamie. The roar overhead had
increased, some vent had been found, and the attic was
in full flagrance. Now, drawing a long breath at the
door near the level of the ground, she returned to her
brother, and disengaged his foot from the slate, then
dragged, then thrust, sometimes at his head, sometimes
at his side; then again she had her arms round him,
and swung herself forward to the right knee sideways,
then brought up the other knee, and swung herself
with the dead weight in her arms again to the right,
and thus was able to work her way nearer to the door,
and, as she got nearer to the door, the air was clearer,
and she was able to breathe freer.

At length she laid hold of the jamb with one hand,
and with the other she caught the lappet of the boy's

coat, and, assisted by the support she had gained, was able to drag him over the doorstep.

At that moment past her rushed a man. She looked, saw, and knew Coppinger. As he rushed past, the blood squirting from his maimed right hand fell on the girl, lying prostrate at the jamb to which she had clung.

And now within, a red light appeared, glowing through the mist as a fiery eye; not only so, but every now and then a fiery rain descended. The burning tobacco had consumed the boards, and was falling through in red masses.

Judith had but just brought her brother into safety, or comparative safety, and now another, Coppinger, had plunged into the burning cottage, rushed to almost certain death. She cried to him as well as she could with her short breath. She could not leave him within. Why had he run there? She saw on her dress the blood that had fallen from him. She went outside the hut and dragged Jamie forth, and laid him on the grass. Then, without hesitation, inhaling all the pure air she could, she darted once more into the burning cottage. Her eyes were stung with the smoke, but

she pushed on, and found Coppinger under the open
window, fallen on the floor, his back and head against
the wall, his arms at his side, and the blood streaming
over the slate pavement from his right gashed wrist.
Accident or instinct—it could not have been judgment
—had carried him to the only spot in the room where
pure air was to be found, and there it descended like
a rushing waterfall, blowing about the prostrate man's
wild, long hair.

"Judith!" said he, looking at her, and he raised his
left hand. "Judith, this is the end."

"Oh, Captain Coppinger, do come out! The house
is burning. Quick, or it will be too late."

"It is too late for me," he said. "I am wounded."
He held up his half-severed hand. "I gave this to
you, and you rejected it."

"Come—oh, do come—or you and I will be burnt!"

In the inrushing sweep of air both were clear of the
smoke and could breathe.

He shook his head. "I am followed. I will not be
taken. I am no good now—without my right hand. I
will not go to gaol."

She caught his arm, and, tearing the kerchief from

her neck, bound it round and round where the veins were severed.

"It is in vain," he said. "I have lost most of my blood. Ju!"—he held her with his left hand—"Ju, if you live, swear to me—swear you will sign the register."

She was looking into his face—it was ghastly, partly through loss of blood, partly because lighted by the glare of the burning tobacco that dropped from above. Then a sense of vast pity came surging over her along with the thought of how he had loved her. Into her burning eyes tears came.

"Judith," he said, "I made my confession to you—I told you my sins. Give me also my release. Say you forgive me."

She had forgotten her peril, forgotten about the fire that was above and around, as she looked at his eyes, and, holding the maimed right arm, felt the hot blood welling through her kerchief and running over her hand.

"I pray you! oh, I pray you, come outside. There is still time."

Again he shook his head. "My time is up. I do not want to live. I have not your love. I could never

win it—and if I went outside I should be captured, and
sent to prison. Will you give me my absolution?"

"What do you mean?" And in her trembling
concern for him, in the intensity of her pity, sorrow,
care for him, she drew his wounded hand to her, and
pressed it against her heaving bosom.

"What I mean is—can you forgive me?"

"Indeed—indeed I do."

"What—all I have done?"

"All."

She saw only a dying man before her, a man who
might be saved if he would, but would not, because
her love was everything to him, and *that* he never,
never could gain. Would she make no concession to
him? Could she not draw a few steps nearer? As
she looked into his face, and held his bleeding arm to
her bosom, pity overpowered her—pity, when she saw
how strong had been this wild and wicked man's love.
Now she truly realized its depth, its intensity, and its
tenderness alternating with stormy blasts of passion, as
he wavered between hope and fear, and the despair
that was his when he knew he must lose her.

Then she stooped, and the tears streaming over her

face, she kissed him on his brow and then on his lips, and then drew back, still holding his maimed hand, with both of hers crossed over it, to her heaving bosom. Kneeling, she had her eyes on his, and his were on hers—steady, searching, but with a gentle light in them. And, as she thus looked, she became unconscious, and sank, still holding his hand, on the floor.

At that instant, through the smoke and raining masses of burning tobacco, plunged Oliver Menaida. He saw Judith, bent, caught her in his arms, and rushed back through the door.

A moment after and he was at the entrance again, to plunge through and rescue his wounded adversary, but the moment when this could be done was past. There was an explosion above, followed by a fall as of a sheet of blue light, a curtain of fire through the mist of white smoke. No living man could pass that. Oliver went round to the window, and strove to enter by that way. The man who had taken refuge there was still in the same position, but he had torn the kerchief of Judith from the bleeding arm, and he held it to his mouth, looking with fixed eyes into the falling red and blue fires and the swirling flocks of white smoke.

There were iron bars at the window. Oliver tore at these to displace them.

"Coppinger!" he shouted, "stand up—help me to break these bars!"

But Coppinger would not move, or possibly the power was gone from him. The bars were firmly set. They had been placed in the windows by Coppinger's orders, and under his own supervision, to secure Othello Cottage, his store place, against invasion by the inquisitive.

At length Oliver succeeded in wrenching one bar away, and now a gap was made through which he might reach Coppinger, and draw him forth through the window. He was scrambling in when the Captain staggered to his feet.

"Let me alone," said he. "You have won what I have lost. Let me alone. I am defeated."

Then he stepped into the mass of smoke and falling liquid blue fire and dropping masses of red glowing tobacco. A moment more and the whole of the attic floor, with all the burning contents of the garret, fell in.

CHAPTER LIV.

SQUAB PIE.

NEXT morning, at an early hour, Judith, attended by
Mr. Zachary Menaida, appeared at the rectory of S.
Enodoc. She was deadly pale, but there was decision
in her face. She asked to see Mr. Desiderius Mules in
his study, and was shown into what had, in her father's
days, been the pantry.

Mr. Menaida had a puzzled look in his watery eyes.
He had been up all night; and indeed it had been a night
in which few in the neighbourhood had slept, except-
ing Mr. Mules, who knew nothing of what had happened.
The smugglers, alarmed by the fire at Othello Cottage,
and by the party collected by Mr. Menaida to guard
the descent to the beach, had not ventured to force their
way to the cave. The *Black Prince*, finding that no

signal was made from the ledge above the cave, suspected mischief, heaved anchor, and bore away.

The stupefied members of the Preventive service
were conveyed to the nearest cottages, and there left
to recover. As for Othello Cottage, it was a blazing
and smoking mass of fire, and till late on the following
day could not be searched. There was no fire-engine
anywhere near, nor would a fire-engine have availed to
save either the building or its contents.

When Mr. Mules appeared, Judith said, in a quiet
but firm tone, " I have come to sign the register. Mr.
Menaida is here. I do it willingly, and with no con-
straint."

" Thank you. This is most considerate to my
feelings. I wish all my flock would obey my advice
as you are now doing," said the rector, and produced
the book, which Judith signed with trembling hand.

Mr. Desiderius was quite ignorant of the events of
the night. He had no idea that at that time Captain
Coppinger was dead.

It was not till some days later that Judith understood
why, at the last moment, with death before his eyes,
Coppinger had urged on her this ratification of her

marriage. It was not till his will was found that she understood his meaning. He had left to her, as his wife, everything that he possessed. No one knew of any relatives that he had, for no one knew whence he came. No one ever appeared to put in a claim against the widow.

On the second day, the remains of the burnt cottage were cleared away, and then the body of Cruel Coppinger was found, fearfully charred, and disfigured past recognition. There were but two persons who knew that this blackened corpse belonged to the long-dreaded Captain, and these were Judith and Oliver. When the burnt body was cleared from the charred fragments of clothing that were about it, one article was discovered uninjured. About his throat Coppinger had worn a silk handkerchief, and this, as well as the collar of his coat, had preserved his neck and the upper portion of his chest from injury such as had befallen the rest of his person. And when the burnt kerchief was removed, and the singed cloth of the coat-collar, there was discovered round the throat a narrow black band, and sewn into this band one golden thread of hair encircling the neck.

Are our readers acquainted with that local delicacy entitled, in Cornwall and Devon, Squab Pie? To enlighten the ignorant, it shall be described. First, however, we premise that of squab pies there are two sorts, Devonian squab and Cornish squab. The Cornish squab differs from the Devonian squab in one particular; that shall be specified presently.

How to make a Squab Pie:—Take ½ lb. of veal, cut into nice square pieces, and put a layer of them at the bottom of a pie-dish. Sprinkle over these a portion of herbs, spices, seasoning, lemon-peel, and the yolks of eggs cut in slices; cut ¼ lb. of boiled ham very thin, and put in a layer of this. Take ½ lb. of mutton cut into nice pieces, and put a layer of them on the top of the veal. Sprinkle as before with herbs and spices. Take ½ lb. beef, cut into nice pieces, and put a layer of them on top of the mutton. Sprinkle as before with herbs and spices. Cut up half a dozen apples very fine, also half a dozen onions, mix, and proceed to ram the onions and apples into every perceivable crevice. Take half a dozen pilchards, remove the bones, chop up, and strew the whole pie with pilchards. Then fill up with clotted cream, till the pie-dish will hold no more. [For

Cornish Squab:—Add, treated in like manner, a cormorant.] Proceed to lay a puff-paste on the edge of the dish. Then insert a tablespoon and stir the contents till your arm aches. Cover with crust, or ornament it with leaves, brush it over with the yolk of an egg, and bake in a well-heated oven for one or one and a half hours, or longer, should the pie be very large [two, in the case of a Cornish Squab, and the cormorant very tough].

In one word, a squab pie is a scrap pie. So is the final chapter of a three-volume novel. It is made up, from the first word to the last, of scraps of all kinds, toothsome and the reverse.

Now let the reader observe—he has been already supplied with scraps. He has learned the result of Mr. Menaida's collecting men to assist him against the smugglers ; also of his expedition along with Judith to the rectory of S. Enodoc ; also he has heard the provisions of Captain Coppinger's will, also that this will was not contested. He has also heard of the recovery of the Captain's body from the burnt cottage.

Is not this a collection of scraps cut very small ? But there are more, of a different character, with which this chapter will be made up, before the pie-crust closes over it with a flourishing "Finis" to ornament it.

Mr. Scantlebray had lost his wife, who had been an ailing woman for some years, and, being a widower, cast about his eyes for a second wife, after the way of widowers. There was not the excuse of a young family needing a prudent housewife to manage the children, for Mr. Scantlebray had only one daughter, who had been allotted by her father and by popular opinion to Captain Coppinger, but had failed to secure him. Mr. Scantlebray, though an active man, had not amassed much money, and if he could add to his comforts, provide himself with good eating and good drinking, by marrying a woman with money, he was not averse to so doing. Now, Mr. Scantlebray had lent a ready ear to the voice of rumour which made Miss Dionysia Trevisa the heiress who had come in for all the leavings of that rich old spinster, Miss Ceely, of S. Austell, and Mr. Scantlebray gave credit to this rumour, and, acting on it, proposed to, and was accepted by Miss Dionysia.

Now when, after marriage, Mr. Scantlebray found

out that the sweet creature he had taken to his side
was worth under a quarter of the sum he had set down
at the lowest figure at which he could endure her, and
when the late Miss Trevisa, now the second Mrs.
Scantlebray, learned from her husband's lips that he
had married her only for her money, and not for her
good looks or for any good quality she was supposed to
be endowed with, the reader, knowing something of the
characters of these two persons, may conjecture, if he
please, what sort of scenes ensued daily between them ;
and it may be safely asserted that the bitterest enemies
of either could not have desired for each a more unenvi-
able lot than was theirs.

Very shortly after the death of Captain Coppinger,
Judith and Jamie left Bristol in a vessel, with Uncle
Zachie, bound for Lisbon. Oliver Menaida had gone
to Oporto before, to make arrangements for his father.
It was settled that Judith and her brother should live
with the old man, and that the girl should keep house
for him. Oliver would occupy his old quarters that
belonged to the firm in which he was a partner.

It is a strange thing—but after the loss of Coppinger,
Judith's mind reverted much to him ; she thought long

and tenderly of his consideration for her, his patience
with her, his forbearance, his gentleness towards her,
and of his intense and enduring love. His violence she
forgot, and she put down the crimes he had committed
to evil association, or to an irregulated, undisciplined
conscience, excusable in a measure in one who had not
the advantages she had enjoyed of growing up under
the eye of a blameless, honourable, and right-minded
father.

In the Consistory Court of Canterbury is a book of
the marriages performed at the Oporto factory by the
English chaplain resident there. It begins in the year
1788, and ends in 1807. The author has searched this
volume in vain for a marriage between Oliver Menaida
and Judith Coppinger. If such a marriage did take
place, it must have been after 1807, but the book of
register of marriages later than this date is not to be
found in the Consistory Court.

Were they married?

On inquiry at S. Enodoc no information has been
obtained, for neither Judith nor the Menaidas had any
relatives there with whom they communicated. If
Mrs. 'Scantlebray ever heard, she said nothing, or—

at all events—nothing she said concerning them has been remembered.

Were they ever married?

That question the reader must decide as he likes.

FINIS.